HANDY

JESSA JAMES

GET A FREE BOOK!

Join my mailing list to be the first to know of new releases, free books, special prices and other author giveaways.

http://freehotcontemporary.com

Handy: Copyright © 2020 by Jessa James

All Rights Reserved. No part of this book may be reproduced or transmitted in any form or by any means, electrical, digital or mechanical including but not limited to photocopying, recording, scanning or by any type of data storage and retrieval system without express, written permission from the author.

Published by Jessa James
James, Jessa
Crave

Cover design copyright 2020 by Jessa James, Author

Design credit: Cosmic Letterz

Publisher's Note:
This book was written for an adult audience. The book may contain explicit sexual content. Sexual activities included in this book are strictly fantasies intended for adults and any activities or risks taken by fictional characters within the story are neither endorsed nor encouraged by the author or publisher.

This book has been previously published.

CHAPTER 1

Derek

"Karen, you can't be serious?"

"I thought you'd be pleased? Why are you acting like this is a bad thing?"

"Because you're giving me no notice!"

"Fine. If you don't want to look after your own daughter then I'll just ask my mom."

I kneaded my temple and quickly found a spot to pullover. Talking to my ex while operating a vehicle was a recipe for disaster. I'd actually be more inclined to run myself into oncoming traffic just so I didn't have to listen to her voice anymore.

"That's not fair, Karen. You know how much I've wanted Kadee to come here. It's always next summer or something came up. It's been years since she's been here but that's not for lack of trying on my part. I wanted to take her up to the lodge but of course you put your foot down, I wanted her to spend time with my parents. But now you want me to drop everything just so you can go on a honeymoon you didn't even have the courtesy of telling me about?"

"Derek, I've just been so busy. I meant to tell you, I really did. You know how hard and time-consuming planning a wedding can be. God, you didn't even say congratulations."

"Congratulations," I said through gritted teeth.

"So? Can you take her? I can put her on a plane tomorrow."

"Wait, what? Alone? You're going to put my baby girl on a plane all by herself?"

"Well, yes. It's perfectly safe! The airline will take care of her. All you have to do is meet her at the gate. Besides do you think Brian or I have time to travel across the country and get back in time for our own flights?"

I could feel every muscle in my body clench, becoming rigid with each word she uttered. I muted the call on my truck's console and let loose a shout of frustration. I was way past boiling point, but this was how it always was with Karen.

"Derek, are you still there?"

My nostrils flared as I took several deep breaths before tapping the screen. "Yes, I'm still here."

"So? I need an answer now. Otherwise I'll have to make alternative arrangements."

The thought of my baby girl spending more time with her ageing grandmother who could barely get around and look after herself or worse still letting Brian's parents take her was not a something I could allow.

"I already said yes, Karen."

"No you didn't."

"Yes I did, you just don't listen."

"Well maybe if you hadn't started shouting at me and practically calling me a terrible mother—"

I wanted to tell her right there and then that she was exactly that but knew the chance of seeing Kadee would most likely go down the drain if I did. Karen loved to use our daughter to punish me.

Instead I managed to rein in the impulse and calmly said, "Text me the flight details and I'll be there at the gate."

"It's tomorrow—"

"Tomorrow? Jesus, Karen," I shouted. "Fine, I'll make it work."

I was about to ask if Kadee was there to talk to and tell her I would be seeing her tomorrow when Karen, with a curt thank you, hung up.

"Bitch!" I shouted at the console.

Taking a deep breath I let the news sink in. Kadee would be here tomorrow. Regardless of the shitty reasons I would have my daughter for longer than I'd ever had before. There was nothing for it but to embrace the opportunity. This could be an amazing two weeks, though I had only the rest of the day to prepare. I would have to rush.

I pulled the truck away again looking to swing around and head back into town. I had to brake abruptly as a speeding SUV hurtled past horn blaring.

"Damn you Karen, why do you always mess things up!"

CHAPTER 2

Georgie

For once my dreams were coming true. Countless hours working over time selling my online designs, as well as a bittersweet windfall, I'd scraped together enough money and it was finally happening. My very own house! So many sacrifices had been made, so much I'd gone without. Several times I'd had to put that extra pint of ice-cream back, or skip over a fun night out, and I certainly hadn't had a vacation in years. I'd already seen a vast majority of the world growing up, I didn't feel like I was missing out too much.

But this was all worth it.

The Victorian styled house in front of me was a little on the plain side, slightly worse for wear, but it was all mine. I leaned against my equally run-down truck and couldn't help but stare up at the structure. Impatient, I'd left the city and my friend's couch and driven straight over stopping only momentarily in my new town of Hollow Point for a few supplies, needing to to get settled right away.

There was so much to do. I didn't even have a bed and would have to rough it for a short while. I didn't care though; I still couldn't believe the house was all mine. And I could already imagine myself in the evenings, sitting on the covered front porch, a cup of tea in one hand and a good book in the other.

This was it, this was how my life was meant to be.

Behind me across the road, I turned to see a blue truck pull into the driveway attached to the house opposite. In comparison that house and plot made mine look like a run-down shack. But soon enough I'd have it gleaming and sitting pretty like its counterpart opposite, here at the end of the cul-de-sac.

I smiled and waved to my new neighbor as he left his vehicle. He was broad and dressed in a red and black plaid shirt that seemed to hug his frame with no breathing room to spare. His tight worn jeans left little to the imagination too. Two sizes too small, not that I was complaining about the two perfect buns or thighs that could crack walnuts which were straining the heavy fabric. Perhaps my new future friend didn't have much luck in the laundry department.

"Hi!" I greeted warmly, and increased the wattage of my smile instinctively as he turned to face me. He was pin-up gorgeous, the type you'd find in those calendars done for charity, each page filled with a half naked fireman or buff soldier. My neighbor had short chestnut brown cropped hair and broody dark eyes, he was pulling a tool bag from the back of the truck. I pictured him as the burly naked handy man of the calendar.

But then he took one look at me and scowled. Maybe he hadn't heard me properly? And like a fool I kept on waving and said hello again. There was no mistaking my greeting this time around.

I was about to make my way over and introduce myself when the man grunted something—which I was pretty sure wasn't anything nice—slammed his truck's door and walked toward his house.

Not even a hello?

I stopped waving, my arm still in the air, and watched him go. In a few strides he was up on his porch, disappearing inside. The front door crashed closed. Clearly looks didn't automatically equate to niceness. *What a dick!*

He'd definitely seen me, right? Not like you could miss someone standing in the middle of the street hollering at you. I almost wanted to go knock on his door to make sure that I hadn't suddenly turned invisible. But quickly shut that thought down. There was no need to get worked up about it. I mean everyone had a bad day once in a while. Yeah that was probably it. I should cut him some slack, even if he had been a grade A jerk. I pushed the thought of my moody handsome neighbor aside and studied my precious new property again.

I had my work cut out for me, and I wasn't going to get anywhere by standing out in the street. The sooner I got started the sooner I'd have a cute little garden brimming with welcoming blooms out front that I could admire from the porch-swing I'd always wanted.

From my truck I picked up the first of the boxes, selected the right key from the small bunch the realtor had given me, and took a deep breath. The path needed weeding I noticed and the paintwork on the porch banister was flaking off. But it was all cosmetic. An easy fix.

Suddenly the smile slipped from my face and I let out a scream when my left foot disappeared, going right through the second step of the wooden porch. Maybe I had developed superpowers.

The box tumbled from my arms and the keys went flying through the air. I braced myself for the inevitable fall and collapsed in a dusty heap, splinters making homes for themselves in my palms. I hissed like a cat at the stinging pain.

The distinctive earthly smell of rot wafted into the air and suffocating dust motes flew around my head. I coughed. The wind partly knocked out of me, all the while my leg, up to my knee, remained trapped between the planks.

Shit. This wasn't the start to my new life that I had in mind.

IT TOOK a painful amount of time to extricate myself from the porch, because each time I moved or shifted my weight the threatening creak of the timbers beneath my trapped body terrified me. I knew if I wasn't careful I was likely to end up falling all the way through. Lost forever in the dark. Would my body even be found, I thought grimly? It was almost felt like the house had come alive and was trying to eat me whole.

I debated whether or not to call for help. Surely my neighbor would take pity on me and come to my rescue? But then I remembered the rude way he'd looked at me and thought better of it. I didn't need *his* help.

Eventually I crawled free, picked some of the splinters that I could see from my hands, and started on the task of finding the keys. I'd lost track of where they'd flown off too. I took one look at the long straggly uncut grass in the front and just knew they'd be in there, somewhere.

With a groan I inched down the porch steps, making sure to keep to the sides—I didn't know how far the rot extended—and started the impromptu treasure hunt.

The sun was setting on Chestnut Grove and the streetlights

did not help illuminate the shadowy depths of the long grass. It felt like forever searching back and forth and I still hadn't found them, thankfully it was a relatively warm night and I wasn't in danger of freezing to death. With my puny little torch light on my phone I scoured the ground, careful not to step into the little presents some critters had left behind.

"Late night weeding?"

Startled I spun to the sound of a voice coming from the sidewalk. I saw the familiar red and black pattern from earlier; my neighbor standing under the weak yellow street light.

"Not quite," I replied gruffly wanting to pay him back for his own rudeness earlier, and returned to my task. I wanted nothing more than to find my keys, get inside, unpack some essentials, shower the day from me and go to bed. Tomorrow I'd start fresh, start again. The mishaps of today were simply a little bit of bad luck. Nothing to be overly worried about.

"Whatever you are looking for you aren't going to find it with that light. It's no better than a flickering firefly."

"Yeah, well, it's all I have," I replied and stood up placing my hands on my lower back to soothe the ache that had been getting increasingly worse. Irritated I turned to *Dick*. "Is there something I can help you with?"

"With that attitude, nothing," he said. *Dick* shrugged and stepped of the sidewalk presumably to go back to his fully intact, perfect little rot-free house.

Then I spotted something in his hand. A rather industrial looking black cylinder.

"Wait." Quickly before he could get across the road I caught up to him. I pointed to the object in his hand. "Is that a flashlight?"

"Depends," *Dick* quipped.

I frowned. What kind of answer was that?

"It either is or it isn't!"

"Now it's definitely not one."

Before I could make myself see sense—he was practically twice my size and a stranger to boot—I lunged for the torch he clearly had in his hand.

"Woah there."

The bastard actually smiled and like a child that did not want to give up his toy he put it out of reach. His arm went vertical, sticking up in the night air with the huge torch clamped in his meaty fist.

Instinctively I jumped for it. I didn't even come close.

"Give it up, you know I need it. The sooner you help me out the sooner you can go home and brood some more."

He laughed again and I almost kicked him in his shins.

"Come on, dude, you obviously saw that I needed help and came out to give me that, right? Being neighborly and all?"

He shrugged.

"Okay you want me to beg? Please, can I borrow your flashlight? I lost my keys and all I want to do is go inside and sleep… this hasn't been the greatest day, you know?"

Slowly his arm sagged a little, he no longer had it locked in place and gravity began to help me out a little.

From the look on his face, he clearly did not want to help me. His stubborn eyes flicked from my face to my house behind me. I took my chance while he looked away and jumped again, this time reaching the target and catching him off guard. I yanked the torch out of his hand and sprinted away.

"Hey!"

I had no idea what I was thinking, it was foolish and silly, it wasn't like he wouldn't be able to catch up to me to get it back. But nonetheless I clicked the torch on and was momentarily dazzled by the blinding white light as I ran towards my patch of grass.

In seconds with the help of the torch that seemed to be powered by the sun I found the keys, glittering in a tuft of turf. "Yes!" I exclaimed and scooped them up tight in my hand. I swirled around to find *Dick's* unamused face, glowering at me.

Trying to diffuse the situation I smiled. "Thanks, I found them. You can have your torch back now."

"Oh really I can? Gee, thank you."

"There's really no need to be so rude. I said thank you!"

"Yeah after you stole my torch!"

"You were going to give it to me anyway!"

"Says who?"

"Oh, whatever. Here take it back. You're the worst neighbor ever!" I took a step toward him about to thrust the damn thing at him, but actually I really wanted to throw it at his face. But I didn't look to see where I was going, I'd shut off the torch and was suddenly blinded by the blackness, the absence of light, and failed to see the loose stone from the path.

"Shit," I said as my foot caught the edge and I let go of the torch. Everything around me seemed to slow down, time almost stopping as the seconds came to a halt. All but the torch froze, that instead was still moving, spinning in the air but slowly but surely getting closer and closer to the ground.

I tried to reclaim it—so did he—we both reaching out and lunged toward the tumbling item. But no matter how hard I stretched, my fingertips never came close. Time unpaused and we were on a collision course. We bounced into each other and for the second time that day I landed in a heap. This time however, it was in the arms of a handsome but surly stranger.

For a second I made the mistake of looking at him properly and I felt a rush of blood thud wildly to my head.

Frozen I could only stare at my neighbor, my eyes adjusting to the surroundings. Even in the dim light I could see his eyes properly now, pools of rich chocolate that could melt anyone's heart. Granted he was the most annoying guy I'd ever met but my body reacted to him in a way that had me licking my lips and flushing like a teenage girl on a first date.

There was a loud crash, the sound of glass shattering as the torch landed hard. I prayed that the thing was robust enough to handle a short fall otherwise mister grumpy was not going to be happy with me.

I slipped free of his arms and gauged my neighbor's reaction, giving him a sidelong glance as I reached my feet and brushed myself off. If he could produce steam from his ears, I think he would've. He was in danger of damaging his teeth too the way he was clenching his jaw.

"Oh crap. I'm sorry… I tripped and it just slipped."

He grabbed his torch off the ground, clicking the switch several times and whacking it against his hand before realizing it wasn't going to turn on.

"Well good work, you couldn't just give it back could you? You just had to go and break it," he growled.

"What! Look, I'm really sorry. I didn't mean—"

"No, we're done here, stop talking."

"I'll buy you a new one, take it easy."

"Just shut up will you!"

Taken aback I returned his stare. "Look, whatever your name is… Who the hell do you think you are telling me to shut up? I said I'm sorry and if you can't accept an apology then my first impression of you was right—"

"Whatever, you're a mouthy little thing aren't you?"

"Eugh! And you're a dick with capital D!" I said and threw my hands up in the air. I couldn't win with this guy, he was the most annoying person I'd ever met, and that was saying something considering I'd spent years around cocky tough guys only out to prove themselves. The longer I was in his presence the more I either wanted to hit him, or jump his bones. There was something wrong with me. Why were all the hot ones jerks or already taken?

Choosing to do neither I retreated to my house, ignoring the calls about replacing his damaged flashlight that were coming from behind.

"Yeah, I have bigger problems to worry about than your dumb five dollar torch, mister!" I shouted back.

Gingerly I found my way up the stairs and across the porch and finally let myself into my house for the first time.

CHAPTER 3

Derek

I checked my watch once again. Kadee's flight had landed and I paced at the quiet gate for a glimpse of her. My sweet Kadee, the daughter I'd not seen in so long. She was still learning full sentences the last time I had seen her, but now was an entirely different matter. During our brief opportunities on the phone or Skype, that Karen had occasionally allowed, she was a proper little person, all questions, full of curiosity and wonder.

Regardless of the aggravating cause of this visit I had to make the most of the time I'd been granted. I would get to to know my daughter and hopefully we could forge a strong relationship for the future. I just hoped my heart wouldn't break in two when I would have to send her back to her mom.

I'd made the airport in plenty of time, time enough for the coffee I had missed this morning. It had also offered me the chance to browse the soft toys that caught my eye in one of the gift shops. Surely a bear would be suitable, but I just didn't know where Kadee's preference lay anymore. Was she still clinging to her favorite thread-worn blanky? Did she even like bears and stuffed toys? There was so much to learn about the daughter that had been cruelly taken away from me.

"Kadee," I called out the moment I saw her, brandishing the bear in my waving arm.

The sight of this slightly forlorn little girl, by the side of an airport attendant, making her way amongst the jostling travelers towering above her made the anger I felt for Karen rear its ugly head.

Kadee looked like she was about to topple over from the weight of her backpack; belongings stuffed into it and which was clearly far too large for a kid her size. How could Karen do this? I had to swallow the anger back down, I was here for the rescue, and I wouldn't take my anger out on my precious girl.

Kadee's eyes darted all around her, searching. I waved again and called her name. A small smile appeared on her angelic face.

"Hey, baby girl." I knelt to welcome her with open arms.

"Hi." Her reply sounded sad, and her hug felt more like a tired surrender. She must be exhausted, I thought and wanted nothing more than to take her in my arms and whisk her away to somewhere safe, but first I had to deal with Kadee's airline chaperone. I handed over my identification and the paperwork was quickly accomplished. She was all mine, at least for a couple of weeks.

"Let's get you home shall we? I have your room all ready. And how about you let me take your backpack?" She nodded and let the weight fall from her shoulders. I stood, hefted it over my arm and took her tiny hand, ready to lead her back to the car park.

"Is that for me, or is it yours?" Kadee asked pointing to the bear I held in my other hand.

"Oh, yes," I replied, completely forgetting the gift which I now offered. "Though he doesn't have a name yet. What do you think his name should be?"

Kadee shrugged but took the fuzzy brown bear into her arms and hugged him to her belly.

"How about Herbert?"

Kadee wrinkled her nose.

"Well, you two can get to know each other before you decide on a name."

Once back at the truck I placed her back pack on the rear seat, and she climbed in the front and buckled up without a word. Each of my inquiries on the journey home were met with little more than shrugs or unenthusiastic "yeahs". She just sat there inspecting the bear in her hands.

I was feeling dismayed after the quiet and awkward journey, maybe once I got Kadee home she could relax. I pulled into the driveway slowly and saw my obnoxious and irritatingly attractive neighbor out of the window. She was fighting with a large box from her overloaded battered truck. This was the first thing to peak Kadee's attention it seemed.

"Who's that?" Kadee asked with a noticeably perkier tone.

"Just the new neighbor, not to worry."

"We should help her out, that's a heavy box."

"I'm sure she doesn't want us interfering at the moment, hon. Let's just get you settled in." I stepped out and went to gather Kadee's belongings from the back.

The clash with my neighbor the previous night had left me wanting to have as little to do with her as possible. But I could already see Kadee marching across towards her.

"Kadee, where are you going? Don't you go troubling her,"

I called after her loud enough so as not to alert my neighbor, but Kadee paid no attention and just kept marching.

"Dammit," I muttered to myself. I slammed the door and walked hastily after her.

I could hear Kadee in full swing as I approached, her voice now confident and cheery.

"Hi. I'm Kadee, welcome to the neighborhood. Would you like some help? My dad can lift boxes. He's strong, don't you think he looks strong?"

"Hi there, and thank you," she replied, obviously taken back a little by the sudden appearance of a five year old by her side.

The neighbor looked a little tired, most likely the result of a rough first night in the new house I imagined. She was wearing casual clothes today, jeans and a long sleeved jersey, ready for a day of action, hauling boxes and doing up the house that should have been mine. I couldn't help but notice the sexy snug fit of the jeans as she bent to dump the large box on the sidewalk, but I tried to avoid catching sight of this, I just wanted to retrieve my daughter and get inside.

"Kadee, you are not to go walking off like that. This may be the end of the road, but it's still dangerous okay? Surely you mom has told you you're not supposed to talk to strangers either?" I scolded her in a stern voice as I arrived at the scene. I could already see the pout forming on Kadee's face.

"I'm Georgie. Pleased to meet you, Kadee. There, I'm not such a stranger now," she replied and shot me a look. Georgie had barely glanced up at me before taking this initiative and undermining my parenting like this. I ground my teeth behind a forced smile. "You have lovely manners, Kadee… unlike some people I know," Georgie added quietly.

"Are we going to help her, Daddy?" Kadee asked as she looked up at me her face innocent and pleading.

"As I said, we shouldn't be bothering the *nice* lady," I replied with as little sarcasm in the "nice" as I could manage.

"But we can help." Kadee was starting to sound adamant. "Well, I'm going to help. What can I carry, Georgie?"

I sighed. It looked like there was no way to tactfully extricate myself at this point without upsetting Kadee. She had taken charge of the situation and had said more words to me in the presence of Georgie than she had on the ride home, so that was something at least. I caught my neighbor's eye with a shared look of resignation and a subtle shrug. Sure those were certainly pretty eyes as they caught the sun here in the daylight, but I wouldn't let myself get distracted, I was just going to do this for Kadee.

"Okay. Let's get this done," I announced. Kadee immediately squealed and dashed off up the neighbors steps.

"Be careful, those steps aren't safe." I shouted after her. This time she listened to my warning and carefully approached the steps, then bent to perch her new bear in the corner.

"She's a delight. I do have to wonder where she gets that from?" Georgie fired off as I turned my attention back to her. I did not honor the remark with a response. If we were going to do this I was going to be civil for Kadee's sake despite the underlying irritation, and irksome attraction.

"Why don't we get all these boxes in and we'll be out of your hair soon enough?"

"Fine."

The box Georgie had been fighting with was indeed heavy, it was labeled books and it appeared to be entirely full. Kadee had already skipped back to the sidewalk and they were both following me toward the house carting suitably sized loads. In Kadee's case this was a couple of shoeboxes. I arrived at the steps and took stock of last nights damage, peering into the hole to access the state of the wood and the supports.

"This looks in fairly rough shape," I called back as I continued up.

I carefully tested the step on the far right hand side and by missing the already broken step ascended to the front door. Georgie was a little to lost in Kadee's questions to respond. Either that or she was ignoring my expert advice. But as I approached the open doorway she called up.

"Every thing's going in the dining room for now. It's on the—" I already knew the dining room was on the left and my deliberate movements had interrupted her directions.

For the next half hour or so, back and forth we went, passing awkwardly and silently at the half way point while Kadee mostly skipped around her new found friend conversing with glee. With the final box in hand I headed up once more. Georgie met me at the bottom of the steps to take transfer of the box. Despite my best efforts, our hands brushed against each other accidentally, hers were soft and warm. Our eyes met for a fraction of a second. Had she felt the same heat spark up her arm as I'd felt? Georgie glanced away and I escaped the moment by quickly launching into a new topic of conversation.

"You would be best stripping all this wood out, and setting new supports in. It looks fairly rotten under there."

Georgie was too busy depositing the final box to reply until she returned to the doorway.

"It'll be fine, I'm sure. Just needs a quick patch before anyone else falls in."

Really, A quick patch? That wasn't the attitude this house needed, or deserved.

"Well sure, but you could lose more of the porch at this rate. It would be well worth seeing to it now, or risk having to do the job more than once. Better to do it right the first time, I say."

"I didn't ask you though, did I?" she quipped. "But hey, thanks for helping with the boxes, I'm good now. I know what I'm doing here."

"If you say so, just trying to offer some advice. But clearly you know what your doing, carry on," I said, my tone dripping with sarcasm. It was obviously not worth persisting at this point or arguing with my stubborn neighbor. I would be wasting my breath getting into what a mistake it would be to patch the porch while the underneath rotted out.

"Come on Kadee, we are done here. Let's go."

"But I don't want to."

"Kadee," I warned but soon caught myself and stopped. I would gain nothing by getting angry at my daughter on our very first day together. "Come on, sweetie, you must be hungry?" I crouched beside her and tickled her belly. She giggled and offered me a small, shy smile.

"What do you fancy? Caviar on toast? Lobster linguini? Chicken cordon blue? Nothing's too good for my little princess," I said with a broad teasing smile.

Kadee giggled again and I spotted Georgie looking too, the apple's of her cheeks rounding out.

"Daddy, don't be silly, I don't like any of those."

"Let's make something you do like then. Anything you want, I'll make it." She slipped her hand into mine and nodded, then turned back to wave goodbye.

"See you later, Georgie!"

CHAPTER 4

Georgie

For the past couple of hours I'd kept myself busy unpacking the boxes for the kitchen. Pulling out what little crockery I had. There wasn't much. A few odds and ends, enough to get by for a little while. I mentally added a trip to the thrift store on my never-ending to-do list for some pots and and pans.

My stomach gave out a grumble and I thought there was no time like the present to christen the haphazard kitchen that certainly would not pass any kind of health inspection. I would make do and prepare some good old homely food while finishing up the last of the unpacking. I hadn't eaten properly since my arrival and my families time honored mac and cheese recipe called to me. I couldn't do too much in the kitchen yet and I only had the few essential ingredients that I had traveled with, my greater culinary adventures would have to wait. Time for a little comfort food.

In the small space, jumping from unpacking then back to the food on the stove I thought about the awkward encounters I'd had with my new neighbor. How dare he stick his nose where it didn't belong? I'd come to learn his name from his sweet daughter Kadee, but Derek Varden was nothing more than an interfering busy-body and a know it all. I couldn't get the smug look he had on his face when he practically chastised me about the porch.

Totally arrogant and overbearing. Not my type at all. Too many years around army bases had cured me of that notion.

First he came over claiming to help, a torch in his hand, only to back away, removing the offer, forcing me to take matters into my own hands. And then the next day he had the audacity to tell me how to fix up my own house? Just because his was perfect and didn't have a porch that was caving in he had to come interfere with mine?

And yet why did my body flush and tremble whenever I was around him? Why did I feel the need to throttle him at the same time as kissing him? I groaned.

As the homely food aroma filled the place I began to question my own behavior each time we'd met. This wasn't really the way I wanted to start things off was it? This was going to be my dream home, where I'd envisaged spending my the rest of my life. Staying put for good. What use was a senseless feud with a neigbor? He had technically only tried to help me since I'd arrived hadn't he? At least from his perspective. Had I overreacted?

By the time I'd finished putting the kitchen items into their suitable places, finding them homes in the now not so dusty cupboards, the food was ready and there was more than enough to feed me for a couple of days. I'd made far too much in my eagerness and decided right there and then that part of the batch was going to be my peace offering; I'd take it over and make nice. We could start over. I just hoped I wouldn't regret my decision.

Confidently I stepped outside, but uncertainty crept back in with each step I took. I was caught between apprehension at how my intrusion would be received and a little nervous at being face to face with Derek again.

His house opposite was a similar style to my new dream home, slightly smaller but with a large garage to the side. The front was very tidy with a tasteful splash of flowering pots. One day mine would look even better I thought, he obviously didn't have the same flare I had.

With one final deep breath I stepped up to the door and rapped loudly with the ornate brass knocker that adorned the front door, then waited. My legs practically shook and I locked my knees. This wasn't a good idea but I willed myself to stay and face the music.

Starting off in a new place with neighbors that hated me was not on my agenda, and I certainly did not want the rest of the neighborhood to get the wrong idea. If this was to be my permanent home after countless years bouncing from town to town, country to country, then I had to make an effort.

After a nerve-wracking long moment the door opened. Derek stood there surveying me with a bemused look on his rugged face. He was clad in a tight white t-shirt with a hint of perspiration on his forehead. He looked positively dreamy, in an all-American kinda way.

"Hi?" he said tentatively mopping his head with the cloth he held.

Even that simple motion flexed his bicep in a very distracting manner.

"Hi, I—er..." I tried to quickly recover from the sudden quickening of my heart. "I brought a peace offering. I don't think we got off on the right foot. Entirely the wrong foot in fact. So I was hoping we could start over? We can forget what happened, actually let's just forget the last twenty-four hours."

Derek seemed reluctant to welcome me in, the door only part way open, his muscle-bound form blocking the way inside. The only reaction I detected in response to my rambling was the slight raising of his eyebrow.

"Of course I still want to make amends for the breakage last night," I quickly added. When he didn't respond I continued rambling on like a fool. "It's just mac and cheese, but I thought it might be good for Kadee too?" I raised the covered dish up higher, letting the comforting creamy scent of my creation waft his way.

His eyes noticeably lit up at this.

"Kadee's taking a nap after the long journey. But I love mac and cheese myself. And I have to admit it smells great."

His unquenchable good manners of his upbringing seemed to be bubbling to the surface in response to my new approach. He was about to reach out to take the dish when he paused.

"Wait, how about you, have you eaten?" he inquired.

"I have plenty, don't worry, I just wanted to—"

"Oh, that wont do, come in. I could definitely use a quick meal and I'm sure you've been busy with the move. There's plenty here, I insist. To making amends?"

This had not been my plan, but his sincere insistence and the hunger I felt at the aroma drove me to accept.

"Okay, sure." I nodded my acceptance as he took the dish and headed back into the house leaving the door wide open.

"Come on through to the kitchen," he called behind him.

I stepped in, closing the door quietly behind me and followed him through the lounge. The place looked amazing even at a glance, there was only a little clutter here and there like on the coffee table; papers, a coloring book, and a few of what I presumed were Kadee's toys. What stood out though was all of the fittings and fixtures around the interior of the house. I'd been studying enough home décor magazines to notice all the immaculate and thoughtful detailing that had been installed in the place. I spied hardwood-trim base boards that must have cost a small fortune. Not to mention the gorgeous crown molding around the windows or the decorative columns that surrounded the edge of the archway through to the dining room. It looked how I imagined my new place being fitted out.

"Your place looks incredible," I called to the sound of plates in the kitchen just ahead.

"Thanks," came the reply as he popped his head back round the kitchen door.

"Have you lived here long?"

"Yeah you could say that. And I've been working on this place for years now. I think I'm just about done. Ready for my next challenge." He looked away as he said the latter, his eyes storming over.

"Seriously, you did all this?" I asked with disbelief, taken back a little by the beauty of the kitchen that met my eyes. "By yourself?"

"No need to sound so surprised, this is what I do."

The casserole dish, plates and cutlery had been arranged welcomingly on the large island; a hardwood top that I longed to run my hands over.

"Please," he said offering me one of the stools to sit at. "Do you want a drink?"

"No no, I'm fine." I said taking a seat and studied the rest of the kitchen, sucking up as much detail as possible. It was an almighty good thing I'd left my phone back at the house otherwise I would've been tempted to take shots of his handy-work and upload them to my Pinterest board.

Derek dished out his own healthy sized portion and

began to tuck in. He seemed much more laid back in his own surroundings, almost adorable. It felt so good to be defusing the tension of our previous encounters. I scooped out a good dollop and joined in, munching on the food.

"This is great," he said through the side of a half chewed mouthful, jabbing his empty fork at what remained of his portion.

"It's a secret family recipe," I joked and smiled. "You've lived here years then, what's the area really like?" I asked, picking a conversation topic that hadn't already brought us into conflict during our brief times together.

He paused his steady intake of food for a moment to consider this.

"It's fairly quiet. Certainly never any trouble, there are some great local places with good people and fair prices that won't gouge you like the city. The cafe down on Main is really good too for a bite to eat, and I think a new place just opened up. Oh and Edgar runs the hardware store if you need it. Which you no doubt will."

"Great, that sounds perfect. How about you two, what's the story with Kadee?" After his obvious hesitation I followed up with, "If you don't mind me asking? You can tell me to mind my own business if you want. I won't hold it against you."

He shrugged, "It's fine. I'm divorced and Kadee lives out west with her mom for the most part. I hardly get to see her."

I decided to tip toe around the emotion creeping into his tone at this new line of discussion.

"That must be tough. She seems like a great kid," I offered in tactful support.

"Yeah, she's everything," he said, sitting back from his empty plate.

He was watching me now with a look I couldn't quite decipher, was it curiosity? Or had I overstayed my welcome?

Before his stare unnerved me too much I continued my questioning.

"And what about you? You said "this is what you do", how do you mean?" I asked gesturing my arms at our surroundings.

"You're full of questions aren't you?"

I took a bite and swallowed. "If you prefer we can sit in silence and eat like two strangers?"

Derek chuckled and shook his head. "Full of sass too."

I smiled. "I try… it's practically the only thing I'm good at."

"I'm sure that's not true. What's your story then?"

"We aren't talking about me. Besides I asked you first."

The edge of Derek's lips curved upwards, the half-smile almost reaching his eyes. "Fine, well, I'm a carpenter by trade. Interior finishings are my specialty you might say, though I've fixed up pretty much everything in this place over the years. You name it, I've fixed it. Maybe I could give you a few tips?"

I bristled at his boastful bravado on this subject and his assumption that I, a *woman*, didn't know what I was doing. And sure his place looked great, but steady on there fella. I was suddenly reminded of our remarks earlier about my porch and his insistence that he knew better. Well there was always more than one way to get something done and this gal needed help from no one! Even if he looked as dreamy as Derek.

"I'll manage just fine, thank you."

Derek shot his hands up. "Suit yourself."

A lengthly and uncomfortable silence sank into the room like an unwelcome fog. Derek glanced at his watch. He tried to do it without me noticing but he wasn't exactly subtle about it either. I shifted on my stool, it squeaked and I winced.

"Are you finished?" Derek asked pointing to what remained of my mac and cheese. There was still a couple of mouthfuls but my appetite had fled.

"Yeah. I'm done. I'll get out of your hair."

"Oh, okay. I'll just clear these up and walk you out, give me a sec."

With my own sudden gush of good manners I reached for the plates to clear up before he had the chance. However without looking it only resulted in me awkwardly grabbing his reaching hand… his warm strong hand. I let out a gasp as sparks zapped up my arm, sending my heart into overdrive for the second time that day.

We froze for a moment, the once relaxed atmosphere of our little mealtime now completely shattered by the intimacy of this touch. I met his eyes for an instant, but before they captured me completely and I surrendered all sense, I broke free. The abrupt motion caused the plate to spin out of control and I could only look on in horror as it careened towards the edge.

Thankfully, Derek had quick reflexes. He shot out his hand, palm flat and managed to subdue the wayward crockery.

"Shit sorry, that was close. I'm not normally this clumsy, I promise."

"Don't worry about it," he said. He sounded annoyed, grumpy and irritated. I'd definitely outstayed my welcome now.

"I should be getting back, I'm expecting a friend soon," I said heading for the door before he could stop me.

"Sure sure, no problem," I heard behind me.

I reached the front door trying to shake the moment off, where I spotted Kadee sat near the top of the stairs, a bear next to her. She was huddled with her arms wrapped around her knees, in the quiet mode of a child who'd sneaked out of bed to listen to the grown-ups talk below. I smiled and sent her a small secret wave. Her little face brightened and she lifted her hand to wave goodbye in response.

Derek had caught up to me and took hold of the door. I left him in the doorway and headed back over to mine. It was perfect good timing as my friend Fiona was just getting out of her car and looking around to see if she had the right place.

"Hey Fee!" I called out to her as I crossed the road.

She looked up a little confused that I had appeared from the wrong side of the road. Fiona was my oldest and only real friend, we had met in college, and even though she had continued through law school while I dropped out we had remained in touch ever since. The fact that she worked in the city an hour away had certainly helped with my decision on the house.

"Hey, I have the right place don't I?" she asked pointed back to my house behind her, "and just who is the hunk, you minx!" she inquired in a quiet voice as I neared.

"Just the neighbor, don't get excited he's a bit of a dick," I said hugging her.

"Well who wouldn't mind a bit of that!" she replied in her usual filthy tone.

"Oh, I've missed you," I laughed. "Come on, let me show you around. See what your scheming has gotten me into."

CHAPTER 5

Derek

"But why can't I go outside, it's so sunny?" Kadee pleaded, her little feet stomping the wooden flooring. Her face started to turn a funny shade of pink as she didn't get what she wanted.

I'd had such a fun morning with her, being woken up by her gleeful face. She'd jumped on the bed and I'd tickled her until she could barely breathe. Hand in hand we'd ventured down stairs and we'd made breakfast together. I was all set to make her favorite; scrambled eggs with toasted soldiers, but it seemed a lot had changed since the last time she'd visited. Now her favorite was pancakes and crispy bacon with lashings of syrup. Yet after our morning fun things were escalating. Note to self: don't get your kid hopped up on sugar first thing in the day. I needed to put the brakes on this little tantrum so I could get some things done around the house and figure out my next project.

"Sorry sweetie, I have some important work stuff to do first," I tried to explain. But you try and convince a sugar-glazed five year old that sometimes you couldn't always have fun all-day nonstop.

"Boring! You're not fun! You're just like mommy! Why can't I go out?" The "I" was drawn out in loud desperation. "I don't have any boring work to do."

"You're not going out on your own, not without me. Not even in the garden. I seem to remember you walking off yesterday to the neighbor's, crossing the road without waiting, despite me telling you not to. That's not happening again, do you hear me?"

Kadee deflated and looked at her feet. Her lips pushed out into a pout and her brows furrowed. She was either going to cry or scream. I braced myself.

"Look sweetie, we'll definitely go outside soon. I won't be long. I promise. I actually have a surprise for you that's coming tomorrow," I said trying to reassure her. But I guess to a kid her age, tomorrow was like waiting for Christmas day that seemed reluctant to arrive.

Thankfully, I breathed a sigh of relief when the seesaw of Kadee's expressions tilted once more. The smile on her face at the mention of a surprise was simply a picture.

"What is it?"

"You'll find that out tomorrow, in the meantime..." I presented her with a copy of *Minions 2* from behind my back. "How about a movie instead, you've only seen the first one right?"

Kadee's eyes lit up further.

"Yes, Mommy said it was stupid so I wasn't to watch anymore," she said with heartbreaking disappointment.

"Well Mommy isn't here now is she?" I said grinning mischievously. "You get comfy on the sofa and I'll set up your movie and get you some snacks. I'll just be in the kitchen on my laptop, okay?"

Kadee nodded, grabbed the blu-ray case and sprinted to the TV. With Kadee settled it was time for me to put my paper work in order and finish up some wood working in the garage. After that I had a couple of invoices to finalize, and a few of phone calls I'd been putting off. Above all I needed to find a new house to buy and renovate for my grand plan to work.

That woman, bloody Georgie, had pretty much ruined everything; sneaking in at the last minute and upping her bid on the house that was supposed to mine. It was suppose to be my ticket out of here, it was going to afford me the chance to be with my daughter, now the mortgage offer I had from the bank was on a countdown to expire. The time it had taken going back and forth with the realtor and the bank was coming back to bite me in the proverbial ass. I had even refinanced my own place in order to put this plan into action. I shouldn't have put all my eggs in one basket. I could have been looking further a field and edging my bets but it had been so perfect; literally right on my doorstep. I would've been able to work on it before and after my daytime handy-man and carpenting jobs that I did around town. Over the street would've been a breeze and I would've been able to get it done twice as fast.

It had all seemed too good to be true… and it was. I should have known something was going to go wrong.

Of all the people that had to win the purchase, she had to be the most infuriating and she did not seem to have a clue. More over, now I had to watch whatever mess she was going to be making everyday as a reminder. It was a travesty really. I had to find a new place and soon, everything was ready. I had saved up supplies and resources, but now not only did I have to find a new house in super quick time, but figure out a schedule where I could work on the house and keep up with my regulars, because the way my luck was going I'd find a house hours away.

With the majority of my paperwork done I set about making another cup of coffee. As I listened to the drip and hiss of the percolator, the quietness of the rest of the house shone through. The movie had finished and Kadee was napping peacefully on the sofa. But the peace and quiet was short lived when I heard some sort of commotion outside. I strained to hear. Was it coming from across the street?

I held the back door ajar to listen to the bangs and shouts. Yep, there was definitely something up judging by the expletives that were being broadcast over the street like angry radio waves. I shook my head and let out a long breath. *Don't interfere. It's not your problem...*

With one more high pitched scream I couldn't take it any longer. I checked on Kadee napping on the sofa and started to head on over. Kadee would be fine sleeping I just had to check things out. For my own sanity really.

There was no answer when I knocked on the door. Georgie—or someone she was potentially beating into submission—sounded in real trouble so I tried the door. It was open and I darted in, following the sounds. I didn't have to go or look far… water sloshed under my feet.

Georgie was crouched in her kitchen. She was drenched from top to toe. Water was spraying from under the sink and she looked almost in tears. Though I couldn't be sure what with all the goddamn water. What the hell was she trying to do? Drown herself? Instal a swimming pool in the kitchen?

"What on earth is going on, you need a hand?" I asked already heading for the sink to take stock of the situation.

No more expletives were forth coming, she just waved the wrench she was holding threateningly towards the sink.

"I was trying to… I just wanted to…" she stuttered in cold wet bemusement.

"It's okay, don't panic. We can sort this out," I said doing my best to block the spray with a rag.

"Wait, you're getting soaked too."

"Georgie, is the mains valve not turned off?" I said looking up at her, her usual snarky composure was all but abandoned in this moment. She just blinked her big brown eyes at me, probably the only feature right now that could distract me from the sopping wet white blouse clinging to her.

"How about the electricity? This water's getting everywhere now." There was still little reaction from her.

I stood her up and held her shoulders to shake her. "Georgie! We need to act fast. I can get the water and the fusebox. I want you to grab some towels and turn on any other cold taps in the house. Quick." I took the wrench from her hand. "Are you with me, Georgie?"

This call to arms finally broke her from her reverie.

"Okay, I can do that."

We headed off to our respective tasks, fortunate that I already knew every details of the house and its layout. With everything turned off I returned to meet Georgie back at the sink. The leak had almost abated and she was diligently packing the towels around the area and damning the flood from escaping any further down the hall. Brushing past her I ducked down under the sink to connect the necessary fittings.

"Are you crazy? What the hell were you actually trying to do here?" I shouted out from under the sink. I mean, how clueless could she be? There had been no need for this mess. Just like the steps this was creating more work. Not that I should give a damn, the house wasn't mine, but still.

"So I skipped a couple of steps, I thought I had it," she retorted, her snark creeping back. "Sue me why don't you?"

"Jesus, and there's wiring down here too. It's so dangerous, Georgie. Just going at things like this, half-arsed, not knowing what the hell you are doing, is going to get you or someone else hurt!" I berated her as I fixed the problem, the naivety made me so angry.

There was no more retorts from up above. I bit my tongue and continued attaching the waste disposal unit she'd tried to add on. Once finished I got back up.

We stood there still breathing heavily from the mayhem, water dripping from our hair. She looked positively miserable with the conclusion of the crisis. Hell she had the far away look of a defeated child, who'd just lost at their favorite game. And I hadn't exactly helped by shouting at her.

"Georgie?" I said softly.

She bit her trembling lip. "I'm sure you're right, it was stupid. I was stupid. You could yelling at me," she replied, looking up at me with glossy eyes.

I couldn't stay mad at her for long when she looked like that, all bedraggled yet gorgeous and hell, her soggy clothing left little to my imagination. I had an overwhelming urge to take her in my arms and hold her until her sass came back. Instead I held steady, feet away from her, resisting the temptation to lick the wetness from her lips.

"Listen, I'm sorry for shouting. I'm just glad we got things fixed and you weren't hurt."

"Thanks, I have to admit I'm glad you were here." She leaned forward, catching her breath and reached out to pat my chest as if in thanks.

She paused, stroked my chest, exhaling a little gasp then looked up at me with those big brown eyes.

I was a goner. Done for. Stick a fork in me... I could no longer resist my growing urge. In one crazy movement I took her in my arms, lips descending upon her mouth with no way of stopping. My fingers cradled her head as I finally got my first taste of the spitfire from across the street.

Almost as if I'd breathed life back into her, she responded eagerly. Desperate hands clutching my shirt, tugging me closer, our cold soggy bodies pressing together. No longer did I feel the cold anymore only the heat of our passionate kiss and the reckless fiery urge to claim her.

CHAPTER 6

Georgie

*E*verything started to snowball. I was not sure when or how the day had started going wrong. I had risen early filled with optimism. I had been fixing up bits and bobs around the house. The waste disposal had perhaps been a step too far. But it had led me to this moment in Derek's arms.

The heart pounding panic of the flood now translated to our hard, unyielding kisses. His hot lips overwhelmed any thoughts of the cold of my soaked clothes as our bodies frantically knocked together, as if they were two bits of flint desperately trying to ignite a spark to start a roaring camp fire.

It felt heavenly despite the carnage around us. We swayed and stumbled over the arrayed towels and splashed through the remaining water, until I was pressed against the counter on the opposite side. He held my face and kissed me more. I welcomed his tongue with delight and ran my hands over him.

"Daddy?"

Kadee's quiet voice shocked us both out of our intimacy. He let go of me and we both straightened up awkwardly.

"Kadee, what are you doing leaving the house!" Derek said with concern.

"I'm sorry, Daddy. I couldn't find you so I came to find Georgie," said Kadee sleepily.

"Okay honey, I'm here. There was an emergency."

"You were kissing Georgie," Kadee said matter of factly.

"No, no that was nothing Kadee… It's okay, nothing to see. I just had to fix the waste disposal."

Nothing? I exclaimed to myself. His desire still lingered on my lips and he sounded like it didn't even matter. I'll jam your head in that waste disposal to see if it's working, if you think I'm nothing mister!

Thankfully I didn't say this out loud and clenched my fists instead, staring at him wide eyed.

Derek offered farewell platitudes as he picked up his sleepy daughter. She waved back over his shoulder to me. In my still shocked state I managed a half wave in return.

I was left alone again amid the mess, this was a hell of a set back. The rest of my day would be spent cleaning up. But that wasn't the most pressing thought in my mind. What had just happened between us, it was a kiss I was certainly going to remember. But his reaction once Kadee arrived on the scene infuriated me. Did he really need to flee the scene so rapidly, like what we had done… or were about to do, was something to be ashamed of?

Fuck… so much for *making up* with the neighbor. I'd never meant for it to go that far. At least not consciously.

CHAPTER 7

Derek

The next morning, Kadee's sleepy face burst to life with excitement when I reminded her that today was the day of the surprise. I was glad of it to, anything that would distract me from my encounter with Georgie yesterday, and my daughter's incessant questions about what exactly Daddy had been doing with Georgie in the kitchen. That was a conversation I certainly wasn't ready for.

Fuck, what had I been thinking kissing her? As if there wasn't enough tension and problems in my life right now.

Thankfully, I hadn't seen Georgie since. Yet that didn't stop my thoughts drifting to her again and again. What she was thinking? What was she doing now? Should I go over? I pushed that idea out of my head immediately, along with the prevalent longing to kiss her again.

"What is it, Daddy?" Kadee asked forcing me to concentrate.

"You'll have to wait and see." I led Kadee to the garage door where the surprise awaited, I had never seen her so giddy.

"Okay, close your eyes, sweetie," I insisted. Kadee scrunched her eyes shut dramatically and I flung open the door. The sight of the brand new bike was met with a high pitched squeal. Living with her mom, Karen's city apartment had never offered any opportunity like this for my baby girl. Kadee had sorely been missing out. Kids needed to be able to play outside in the fresh air, riding bikes and climbing trees. Though, one thing at a time. The trees could wait and skinning knees were certainly not on the agenda. It was time to set things right, but with the level of safety my baby girl deserved.

"Now, first things first, Kadee. You'll have to get geared up, even with the training wheels on. Safety first!"

"I don't need training wheels. Just you watch," she said confidently, and grasped the handlebars all read to jump aboard.

"Wait, now. Come here."

Reluctant to leave her new bike Kadee frowned, but with a little encouragement she eventually followed me when I ushered her to the pile of clothing on a bench inside the garage. Her giddiness had been replaced with attentive determination, eyes on her new bike. We got her all kitted out, gloves, pads, and helmet, together with my own little additions. I adjusted some of my own knee pads, I used when laying flooring, to fit her and strapped them on like shoulder armor. I stood back to admire my work. Kadee grinned back from under her large helmet. No harm was going to come to my darling girl.

My truck was parked down the street, leaving the driveway free to use. I walked the bike out to the sidewalk so she could ride toward the garage at first. Kadee waddled alongside me, practically squealing with delight, her hands outstretched wanting to be constantly in contact with her gift.

"Let's do this. Are you ready? Hop on."

Kadee tentatively clambered on as I held the handlebars steady.

"Now you keep your feet on the peddles, okay? And don't let go."

"I know, Daddy. Here I go!" she exclaimed as she rang the bell loudly.

I let go of the handlebars after she got peddling, able to prop her up by the shoulder pads. She wobbled slowly forward as I walked beside, holding on to the underside of the saddle.

"Let go, Daddy, I can do it," she pleaded after one trip back and forth.

"Not yet, you need to get used to it first."

As we arrived back at the sidewalk Georgie's truck pulled up to her house across the street. She got out, looking over with a furrowed brow. Before anyway awkward greeting could be produced from either of us Kadee screamed out. "Georgie, Georgie! Come look, it's my new bike. Do you want to see?"

Georgie smiled at Kadee. "Let me just put these things in house, I'll be out in a moment," she said with little more than a glance at me.

Maybe she thought our kiss hadn't been all that?

I recognized the bags from the local hardware store, more disasters awaited it seemed.

Kadee stubbornly wouldn't set off again until Georgie had returned, when she did we were ready to go again.

"Okay, let's see what you're made of, Kadee," Georgie said standing at the side of the drive ahead of us.

Off we went again as I corrected the wobbles and kept her moving forwards.

"A quick question, Derek. Why is she dressed like a hockey goalie? Is this training for some sort of new extreme sport I've never heard of?" Georgie directed at me as we teetered past her.

"Mock all you want, but my little girl is not getting hurt. That's not how I do things."

"Looks like she's a little too secure. If you're not careful she might roll off down the street should she fall off what with all that padding. She can barely move, that's not riding a bike."

"How about you mind your own business?" I said with a scowl and went back to ignoring her, refocusing on my little cyclist. "How are you doing, sweetie?"

"Georgie's right, I don't think this is riding a bike, you're not letting go," she replied with a sigh.

As if to prove her point, Kadee took her hands off the handlebar and tried to cross them across her well-protected, puffed out chest, but the padding wouldn't let her elbows bend.

Behind me I heard a chuckle. I flashed a glare back at Georgie, her face only returned a look of smugness.

"She's not a test pilot, Derek. She's not on a rocket about to be shot off into space. Nothing's going to happen, she just needs the chance to learn, and for you to let go," Georgie called over as we came to a stand still again at the garage.

"Is that what happened with your sink is it?" I fired back, this woman was incorrigible. And yet my gaze kept ducking down to study her lips every time she opened her mouth. If only I had an excuse to shut her up with another kiss.

"Oh, you know fine well what happened with my sink!" Georgie countered, her eyes flashing, as she bit her lip. I almost groaned for wanting her. "Kadee honey, you should ask your dad if I can help you ride the bike tomorrow. I'll show you how it's really done."

With that Georgie stormed off back across the street, slamming her front door behind her.

"Daddy, I'm tired now and really hot and sticky. I don't think I want to ride anymore today. Not like this." She let out a big breath, her cheeks red.

"But, sweetie you're doing great. We just have to take it slow so you don't get hurt. A few more minutes?" Kadee shook her head. I buried the disappointment, this was not how I planned our day to go. There was nothing more I could do as Kadee took it upon herself to stumble off her shiny new bike then took it from my grasp, wheeling it back into the garage.

I had to remedy this, but how? I had to at least make things amicable again, this was getting rapidly out of hand. Kadee's happiness was everything to me.

"Could I daddy?" Kadee looked up at me with the sadness of a lost puppy, "could I ride with Georgie tomorrow? Please?"

I pondered this for a minute, there was little reason to say no. If it would make my sweet girl happy while she was here, then maybe I should let some slack into the reins. I also had to admit deep down, a part of me did want to be near Georgie again.

"Okay, anything for you," I said and pulled her into a hug. "But I think maybe I have some apologizing to do first. Let's see what we can do about that shall we? How about a little trip into town?"

CHAPTER 8

Georgie

Why was it that every time I saw that man I wanted to jump him, yet we instead got into some kind of shouting match? He was so far under my skin I didn't think the itch would ever leave me. He had the audacity to kiss me in my own kitchen yesterday and then not even say hello. Well fine, I had other things to worry about. Because I knew I wasn't frustrated just because of his attitude toward me.

Having an overprotective father could really dampen a girl's fun. Poor Kadee merely wanted to ride her bike, instead she looked like a tiny version of the Michelin Man. I remembered fondly the hours cycling around the military bases where my father was stationed. A girl needed her wheels, her freedom, even if it was on a secured, fenced-in site with soldiers keeping pace as you rode.

Granted Kadee wasn't at that age yet, or even in the same

predicament that I was. She was in a quiet, leafy cul-de-sac, where the only danger was a pothole in need of repairing. But if Derek was going to keep on wrapping her up in layers upon layers of cotton wool, strapping padding to her like she was part of the defensive line, she'd soon push back. Hard.

Suffocating a scream, I slammed the front door. It rattled and with it the rest of the house. I slumped back against it and as if in response to my turbulent thoughts and the state of my mind, the wooden rack to hang coats and scarves besides the door that looked like it had been installed when the house was first built, clattered to the floor. A dusty shower of plaster snowed down on top of it. I screamed internally, was this whole place falling apart? Had I made a mistake coming here?

I kicked at the dead rack and headed for the dining room where my new purchases waited. Slamming doors, much like that damnable neighbor, may be best avoided.

Needing to occupy my hands, before I wrecked anything else, I emptied the bags, scattering my purchases from the hardware store across the dining room table. There was too much stuff I didn't know what to do with, I'd bought with my heart instead of my head. I had also been busy buying decorative details I couldn't resist but had little chance of putting to use yet.

Studying Youtube videos over the past couple of weeks had made everything look easy enough. But now in the face of the reality of it all, it felt overwhelming. There was so much to do. Maybe Derek was right; I didn't know what I was doing and I didn't know where to start for the best. I hadn't even thought about the porch steps that still needed mending, and the kitchen was still drying out. This surprisingly expensive shopping trip was not going to make much of an impact. Only two days in and the costs were racking up.

Perhaps I shouldn't have spent quite as much on the new bed that was due to arrive later today, but as my aunt had always said, "if nothing else, always make sure you have a decent bed. After a good night's sleep or a roll in the sack, you'll be ready to tackle anything." Doing the horizontal mambo wasn't exactly part of my agenda when I bought the thing, even with the dreamy hunk across the street plaguing my thoughts. But I couldn't bare to sleep another night wrapped up in a sleeping-bag on top of thin sofa cushions.

Thinking of aunt Dakota, and all of her timely advice, somehow revived my determination. I had to start somewhere today, even if it was something small.

Bite by bite, I would get there.

I did not have anything ready for tackling a serious job in the house. But as long as I got going, made a dent in my ever growing to-do list, however superficial, I would hopefully feel better. My mind jumped back to the new hole beside the front door, left by the rack. There was some logic to starting at the front door and working inwards. Before I could talk myself out of it, or let doubts creep in like territorial spiders, I grabbed up the necessary materials, wall filler, a smoothing spatula, damp cloth and got to work with renewed purpose.

AFTER WHAT SEEMED like hours I felt like I was not making much progress, but I was still standing. Teeth set and determined. Starting with the hole the rack had left behind I'd worked around the room patching the walls as I went, smoothing over the rough finish and filling in holes left by picture-frame nails. I had to give myself some credit, it looked a little better. I also felt the weight lift ever so slightly from my burdened shoulders, like I had not only evened out the walls but also smoothed out the frayed edges of my current emotions.

Spying the tatty old shelf in the dining room, I pointed to it with my newly acquired crowbar. "Your time's up!"

It had to go, I couldn't walk past it without scrunching up my nose like there was a bad smell. It had been fixed there with little care or attention with ugly miss matched materials.

It had obviously made itself at home there in its crooked position on the wall and was resistant to the idea of moving. The old rusty screws had given up on their purpose in life long ago and protested when I tried to pry them out. Even when everything that was seemingly holding the shelf to the wall had been removed, it clung there still as if it had fused with the house itself. I laughed, would I have to demolish a whole wall just to get rid of the thing?

"Don't look at me like that, you have to go! We tried the easy way, now for the hard way," I said and plucked up a hammer.

I glared at it for a moment hoping it would finally give up, but I wasn't so lucky. Tentatively at first, I whacked it, my hits getting more furious, rage and frustration channelling their way through the hammer till the point of impact.

But it didn't move. I stood back exasperated and stared at the ugly thing. How was it still clinging on?

In desperation, I took a firm grip of the shelf, letting it bear my weight, and jiggled downward, pulling as hard as I could. At first it didn't budge, but with a final exertion it collapsed.

There was a loud clatter and a crumbling sound as the shelf hit the floor followed by more plaster and dust, then me of course when I couldn't keep my balance. I coughed and cursed in equal measure.

"HA! Georgie 1 - House 0! Now what do you have to say

for yourself?" I said to the mess on the floor accusingly. I supposed technically if we were keeping score I was very much behind, but deluding myself was the better option for the moment, I thought with a wry smile.

There was a firm knock on the door.

I looked from the front door back to the discarded shelf with a raised eyebrow.

"Friends of yours out for revenge?" Dusting myself off I went to answer it, wondering who it could be since I barely knew anyone in Hollow Point.

Derek and Kadee stood there. The sight of him stirred my anger as well as that persistent tingle down below. God, he was so yummy. Especially when he wore that tool-belt around his hips, bearing the heavy weight of the instruments of his trade. Not to mention how it also had the added benefit of pushing the tops of his Levis down a smidge, allowing me a sinful glimpse of the defined contoured muscle that led, I could only imagine, to heaven.

Distracting myself I turned to Kadee's bright smile. She was grinning and holding out a large book. He was also holding a bundle of something.

"Hello?" I greeted them hesitantly, "what's going on?"

"Hi, I was thinking…" Derek started, but trailed off. Was he blushing?

"This is for you!" Kadee blurted out.

"Yeah, that's for you," he continued with a small smile. "And I was thinking it would be pretty great if you would help Kadee tomorrow with her bike. We both agreed. I also never really thanked you for the food the other day."

I took the large book from Kadee's excited hands.

"Oh," I said quite stunned at this turn-around. Maybe he wasn't all hard edges after all? "And what's this" I asked studying the book.

"Well, I think that will be great for you, it's been with me for years. I don't really need it anymore. But you could probably get some use out of it."

It was a heavy robust volume, weathered and worn, and had the feel of a book that had been bound a couple of decades ago. In neat gold lettering on the cover read "Renovation and Home Improvement - The Beginners Path To A Dream Home".

"I know It looks a little old but it's pretty much perfect for houses like this. Especially if you want add those traditional touches."

I was busy dwelling on the word beginner as he explained. Sure I was a novice but did he really see me that way? Like I needed an instruction manual to get by? "Thanks," I said and put the book to one side. It was the thought that counted right?

"I also got you this for you, think of it as a house warming gift, maybe?"

I unraveled the bundle which appeared to be a work belt of sorts. I could feel myself blushing, had he somehow caught my lingering gaze all those times I'd seen him wear his? Continuing to peel back the layers, I peeked inside. There was an array of shiny new tools some of which I didn't even recognize, let alone name.

"Oh, wow. These look expensive. You shouldn't have. Really, I can't accept this."

He waved away my words. "I insist. You'll find them invaluable for anything your doing. Trust me, you'll wonder how you ever got on without them after you give them a try."

It was hard to resist his sincerity and the confident, passionate manner in which he always spoke about his line of work. Though I wished we could talk about that kiss instead, but with Kadee present I bit my tongue and hushed the urge, as well as the persistent warmth to my cheeks.

"Georgie, can we ride my bike tomorrow?" Kadee chirped in, a little bored with the grown up conversation.

"Now hold on Kadee, don't forget your manners. What do you say?" Derek interjected.

Kadee stood up a little taller and in her most endearing voice invoked the magic word like a small but determined wizard.

"Please?"

I looked back to study Derek's expression for a moment, making sure he was completely on board. He nodded and I shot back a smile.

"It'll make her day," he encouraged, "and mine."

I blinked, wondering if he'd actually said those last words or if I'd imagined them.

Kadee tugged on my hand. "So will you?"

"Of course, honey. I'll be there, we'll have so much fun." I glanced back to Derek, our eyes locked. "Come and get me anytime," I said and waited to see his reaction to the potential innuendo.

Derek coughed. "Great, there we go, sweetie." Derek shifted his attention from Kadee back to me. "I'm sure I'll come in handy sooner or later… so let me know if you need any help."

CHAPTER 9

Derek

"Now close your eyes sweetie, time for dreams," I said tucking Kadee in a little tighter with her bear.

I now knew the difficulty in getting her ready for bed when something exciting was on her mind. Even though we'd read three bedtime stories, she had not stopped talking about Georgie and more time with her bike tomorrow. But she was all settled, finally, her heavy eyelids were slowly closing. I lent down and kissed her sleepy head.

"Do you like Georgie, daddy?" she murmured.

"Well, what do you think?"

"I asked you first, but I like her."

"She is very nice." As Kadee's brow furrowed slightly, perhaps not entirely pleased with my tentative answer, I added, "but I do know she likes you."

"Do you think she's pretty?"

"Not as pretty as you, baby girl."

"Daddy! You didn't answer. I'm not going to sleep till you tell me. Properly."

"I think she's very beautiful," I replied, thinking maybe one day my little girl would make a fine interrogator. But I couldn't lie to Kadee, even if it meant acknowledging feelings that had seemingly bubbled up out from nowhere.

I stroked Kadee's fine hair gently, smoothing down the little wispy curls around her forehead. "Now, no more questions, sleep time. You want to be up bright and early to play, don't you?" Kadee nodded, her eyelashes fluttering as she shifted.

Silently I stayed and watched as she drifted off, her breath becoming light as she sank deeper into her pillows. As quietly as I could, I stepped away, careful not to trip over a few toys that hadn't been tidied away, and headed downstairs.

Obviously I hadn't wanted to answer Kadee's question directly, but I couldn't deny what even a five year old could see and had intuited. There was definitely something between us. Electricity practically leapt from my body when Georgie was around. But these days I had with Kadee were precious, I didn't need the distraction. The truth however was clear as day, I found Georgie irresistible, despite the paces she'd put me through.

In fact, her beautiful eyes struck me every time I saw them. I could barely think of anything else, it was as infuriating as her infectious sarcasm. But I couldn't deny the effect Georgie had on me. I also couldn't decide if her sassy character turned me on more than it should, she was certainly feisty.

At least watching her storm away from our numerous conflicts had its benefits. Watching her tight jeans, hips swinging, as she crossed the road had left an impression on me that I had a hard time shifting. *Hard* time indeed, I remembered with a smirk, then immediately scolded myself for my wayward thoughts. I had to get myself together, this was still the same woman who had single handedly wrecked my dreams and plans of buying the house across the street so I could flip-it and finally have enough to afford something remotely decent and suitable out west, closer to Kadee.

I opened a beer from the fridge and settled down to browse Netflix to take my mind off things. The baby monitor I had for Kadee's room sat on the coffee table. Sure she was a little old for such things, but I wasn't going to take any chances. Not with my girl.

After a good while scrolling through the app, unable to finding anything that piqued my interest, I sighed. I didn't feel like watching anything anyway, I was too distracted. I frowned as a I heard a light knocking, and paused to listen. It was definitely the front door. I checked the time, it was getting dark outside. I downed the last of my beer, and got up as a rather raunchy trailer started to auto play on the TV. The idea of a Georgie booty call suddenly jumped into my head. I tried to shake the idea off and opened the door.

Georgie stood illuminated in the porch light. Behind her across the street her house stood in darkness. Her sudden appearance left me speechless.

"Er, hey. I didn't want to disturb you. I just had a quick question really."

"Okay, sure go ahead," I responded swallowing, "is it about the house?" I added to fully dispel the booty call illusion. It didn't matter how long I'd gone without a good-woman in my bed, I couldn't entertain those thoughts, no matter what.

"Well yeah, it's more of a hypothetical question really."

"Hypothetical, sure. Shoot. What's the problem?"

"Let's say you didn't have power in the house, and when

you went to the fuse box it kept tripping. Then let's also say your only source of light—your phone—died because it wasn't charged. So yeah, if this was your hypothetical problem, what would you do?"

I nodded along with her roundabout explanation and scratched my head, indulging her. "Hmm, sounds troubling. In this situation, I don't have a flashlight do I?"

"Ah no, afraid not. The only available torch may have been broken," she smirked as she dropped her coy facade. "So yeah, that's the problem. I'm sure the answer was in the book, but I can't read it in the dark. I was about to start reading in the van but I can't find the keys. It's getting late and I'm super stuck."

The TV-show trailer on Netflix started up again, the sexual sounds heard all the way from the lounge to the front door.

"Though, maybe you have better things to do?" Georgie mocked with a mischievous smile, leaning her head in through the opening inquisitively. "What are you watching? Something R-rated? Fifty Shades of Hardwood?"

Ignoring her question, I didn't answer. Regardless, I don't think I could've without blushing like a fool. "Give me a sec, I'll be right with you." Flustered I went to turn the TV off and gathered up my phone and the baby monitor. "Kadee's asleep but I can come take a look, but only for a minute," I said showing the content of my hands.

"Great, thank you," Georgie said with a smile and turned to leave.

As we strolled across the tranquil street together, I adjusted the flashlight on my phone. The comfortable peace was short-lived, however.

"A baby monitor, really?" she inquired with her characteristic hint of sarcasm.

"Definitely, I'm keeping my girl safe and sound, whatever

it takes. Besides, wouldn't you agree it's proving handy right now?"

She didn't really have time to respond as we navigated up the broken steps and into the dark house.

"Now watch how you go, there may be some mess on the floor," Georgie warned.

The fuse box was toward the rear of the house in a small hallway that led to the back door. As I guided us through the house I aimed the light from my phone at objects and furniture so we could avoid them. Georgie was following close behind me. I could feel her presence, smell her sweet perfume. She was intoxicating. Almost too close… driving me wild.

As we made it deeper inside, it was surprising just how pitch black is was in the back, away from the diffused glow of the streetlights. "Careful, nearly there." Saying it more for my own benefit than hers. Sooner I got this sorted, the sooner I could get back home. Away from temptation.

Once at the fuse box I handed over the phone for her to direct the beam as I investigated the source of the problem. It was a much older circuit breaker, with chunky circular fuses, molded with heavy duty grey plastic. And sure enough it tripped when I threw the mains.

"Of course, we wont be able to find the specific source of the problem in this darkness. But if we can pinpoint which circuit it is we can skip that one to get some of the power back on," I advised.

"Yes, I agree, just what I had in mind," Georgie replied then paused. "How do we do that?"

"Trial and error. I'll remove each one in turn and pass the fuses to you as we go. We narrow it down."

"Sure thing, I'll be right here."

She was indeed right there. The narrow hallway wasn't really built for two people to be in there at the same time. It was more like a cupboard than anything and in this dark confined space I was very aware of her brushing up against me to angle the phone light over my shoulder. I gave out a notable sigh and willed my self control to concentrate on the task at hand.

"Oh no, what's wrong with it?" asked Georgie after a moment. I detected a bit of panic in her voice at the sound of my sigh. She pointed the light from the fuse box into my face.

I squinted at the sudden brightness in my eyes.

"It's fine, just hold that steady will ya? And try not to blind me?"

She laughed and returned the spotlight the fuse box. "I'm not going to drop it you know," she said, nudging me with her elbow.

Given how mad I had been on that first night, she sure knew how to tread a fine line with her jests. Admittedly her manner was growing on me.

"Well, you never know," I retorted. "You and your butter fingers."

Two fuses removed and still no joy, I pulled out the third to hand it over. I hadn't noticed Georgie struggling with the other fuses as well as the phone. The third fuse leapt from her fingers as she shuffled them in her hands. I reached after it, but in the confusion I stumbled into Georgie bending over to reclaim the stray fuse. I knocked into her ass with some force, pushing her forward. Instinctively I grabbed her to steady her from a fall… and fuck, it sure felt good to have my hands on her.

She gave out a small gasp of shock that aroused me further.

Georgie straightened up and turned to face me in the darkness. Her chest rose and fell against me, her heavy and hot breath licking up my neck, testing me. Daring me. I couldn't bear it any longer, the fuse box forgotten and took her in my arms and kissed her.

She moaned under my touch, her lips parted, admitting me entrance. We were lost for a time in our passion there in the hallway, exploring each other's mouths as if we were hunting for lost treasure.

Breathless we parted paused for a moment. "Two secs," I whispered, wanting to be able to see her properly. I reached out to try the mains once more.

To my surprise it didn't trip. We were still in darkness in the hallway, but a glow from the staircase in the main hall filtered across the wooden floor, spilling onto our feet.

"You have some lights, that's a start. I should try and get this finished up," I suggested, my senses returning to me.

"Oh, hell no, not again," Georgie said, her voice low, hands still upon my chest, fingers clawing at me. "You need to take care of something else first." Georgie ran her fingers down my arm and took my hand, pulling me back towards the stairs.

CHAPTER 10

Georgie

"We need to be quick," Derek said, an eager whisper, his hands unable to leave my body, tugging me towards him as we moved through the house.

"Quicker the better," I said smiling over my shoulder.

This hadn't been my plan, it almost felt like a daft story from of porn movie. Handy man comes to the rescue, lights flicker out, the girl get's nailed. Though I couldn't deny that the thought hadn't played over in my mind a few times since we'd met. But this was no dream, and there was no longer any point in fighting my attraction for this man. We obviously wanted each other, and I had a brand new bed upstairs all made and ready for use. Sage advice aunt Dakota, thank you. The rhythmic chords of the mambo started playing in my head.

We kicked off our shoes at the bottom of the stairs and I towed him to the master bedroom, not that he was reluctant.

The landing light provided the right subdued lighting in the bedroom and I didn't flick any other switches… I'd let him do that, I thought with a wicked grin. I deposited the phone and the baby monitor on the dressing table, then glanced over to him. With an almost primal look in his eye he erased the space between us, immediately embracing me again.

He pulled me close to his strong body, the passion in our kisses escalating rapidly. Our hot lips dancing around playful tongues while he edged me closer to the bed with every kiss. I pulled his shirt from his waist and started to fight with the small buttons. He helped with the last few and shook his shirt off onto the floor. My hands pressed onto his exposed muscular form, feeling how solid he was. How very real. I had to wonder how much a man would have to hammer to get arms as thick and strong like this. He didn't seem like the gym type, but he sure as hell looked like he could bench-press me with little effort.

I ran my fingers over every bulge and ripple as he pulled open the buttons on my jeans forcefully. I returned the favor and we efficiently discarded more garments, letting them fly from our bodies. I flung my top across the room dramatically and stood in only my underwear, and watched his eyes, waiting for his next move.

He stepped up to me slowly this time, sliding his arms around to hold all of me, making me shudder with each stroke. Our warm exposed bodies met, skin tingled against skin, as his hands roamed up and down my back.

Inch by inch he backed me toward the bed. Finding that my bra had been unclasped I wriggled out of it, still locked in the safe cocoon of his arms. He brushed against me, his firm chest making my nipples zing and stand up and take notice.

Derek's urgent kisses suddenly strayed to my neck, I couldn't help but murmur pleasurably at his attentions. He kissed the sensitive area slow and steady, his hands sliding all the way down my back. They didn't stop this time and he ran them under my knickers and squeezed my ass tightly. His fondling urged my panties downwards and when he gave them a little tug I obliged by sliding out of them. Not waiting he did the same to his own. I bit my lip and watched as his confined cock was revealed. It revelled in its new found freedom and rapidly stood tall to greet me. Hopelessly needing him, I took matters into my own hands and stroked it lovingly, its girthy length becoming increasingly harder the longer I lavished it with attention.

He advanced on me once more and suddenly we were falling backwards, I collapsed onto the bed and he fell on top of me, one leg between mine, his thigh grazing my apex. Our lips found each other once, our tongues wrestling for control, neither of us giving it up.

With one hand for support he squeezed my breasts, enthusiasm pulsing from his palm, then pinched at each nipple in turn. Again his thigh pressed firmly up between my legs, rubbing me into a frenzy, as we kissed and writhed higher up on the bed. I squirmed against him in delight stroking and clawing at his heavenly body urging him on. I was so ready for him.

Derek shifted his full weight between my legs, spreading me wide, his cock nudging against me.

"Take me please," I purred up at him, stroking his bit of rough on his chin.

Softly he kissed me, and before I knew it he was plunging inside me. I arched my back at the sensation and wrapped my arms around his broad back. He looked deep into my eyes with a desire I did not expect. He paused for a second, his heat growing.

"Jesus, you feel so good," he said then added with a coy smile, "slow or fast?"

"Fast," I replied, my arms wrapping around him, pulling him closer to me.

"Hard?"

"God, yes!"

He grinned as his thrusts, slow at first, quickly grew to a steady insistent pace that was heavenly beyond words. His face vanished into my neck as he nibbled and bit at me, his hand still fondling and pinching my rigid nipples. All of these pleasures sparked fireworks between my legs as he worked me. His body was heavy upon me, and I spread my thighs wider and wrapped my legs around him tightly.

Digging my heels into his ass, he took the hint that I needed more.

"You want this hardwood, huh?"

"Yes! Fucking nail me to the wall..."

He thrust even harder, rocking me further up the bed with the force. The bed shook, the headboard started to bang loudly, punishing the wall.

I began to moan louder, urging him on ready to feel him cum inside me, wanting him to tip me over the edge, detonating inside me. I clung to him tightly whispering into his ear to give it to me harder as he groaned into mine. Forgetting everything I threw my head back, lost in the fierce and rapturous treatment. With easy strength he pulled me up and rolled us over till I was sitting in his lap, his hands cradling my bottom as he continued to fuck me hard. I hung on bouncing upon him, my arms around his neck, our sweaty bodies squashed together as if we were trying to become one.

"I'm so close," I breathed. "Don't stop. Yes, harder!"

He renewed his efforts and I threw my head back again, his lips descending upon my neck, then breasts. My body went rigid, tightness rendering me speechless... Until, with a final scream I came. He came hard too, still plunging deep into me. My body shuddered in response, and I rode a secondary wave of pleasure as he exploded.

He collapsed his full weight on top of me pinning me to the bed. He felt so good, so real. His musky scent was intoxicating, making me lift my chin to kiss his damp skin. Even this moment I didn't want to end. Once he caught his breadth he slumped to the side one leg still entwined with mine. I turned toward him as we caressed each other.

"Well ain't you handy with your hands, as well as your tools," I whispered, grinning at him mischievously.

"And you're so goddamn beautiful," was his response as he lent in to kiss me. "Jesus that was unexpected…"

"If you say so. Guess that kiss in the Great Kitchen Flood of 2018 did mean something, then?" I taunted.

"Yeah, seems like it did," he smiled back at me.

I saw him nervously glance over at the baby monitor as if reminded of Kadee's previous surprise interruption.

"She's fine I'm sure, want to go check on her?"

"In a minute," he breathed.

Wanting to reassure him I lifted my head and said, "Is her room at the front of the house? Because you can see her room from right here."

"Yeah," he answered hesitantly, sitting up on the bed to peer over to the house. It was all quiet and peaceful, so he slumped onto his back on the bed with a deep contented breath. I rolled over to snuggle next to him stroking his chest. "I should probably get back soon, though."

"You should. But in a moment, just a little while longer?"

"Okay," he said and stroked my hair.

"You're a little crazy for that girl aren't you?" I joked in a soft tone.

"Can you blame me? She's amazing. She means the absolute world to me. Even if I hardly get to see her."

"That's not right, a little girl needs her daddy."

"You're telling me. Hell, I could count the times I've seen her in the past two years on one hand. She moved to the west coast with her mother and I didn't have much say in the matter," he said holding up his hand. "I go out there as much as I can but, it's never enough, you know?"

Absent-mindedly I interlocked my fingers into his upheld hand, and we both watched as our fingers intimately played as we talked.

"I was planning on going out there properly, so I could spend more time with her, but then…" he said trailing off as my stomach did a little twist. He couldn't leave, I thought selfishly, not when we'd just found each other.

"Why didn't you?" I asked cautiously.

"Something came up. Best-laid plans and all that," he replied and looked away back toward the house across the street.

"It's understandable you would do it for Kadee but it sucks if you would have to move away. I've moved around all my life and I've had just about enough of that. It feels good to settle down. To finally feel like this is the last bed I'm ever going to rest my head."

"But why Hollow Point. Do you have family here?"

"Nope, my parents are still living their lives, like they've always done. But why not Hollow Point, is my question. It's as good as place as any to put down roots… and the neighbors aren't too bad either."

CHAPTER 11

Derek

*I*f Kadee had been over excitable the first morning with her bike, this time around she was bursting at the seams. She talked about Georgie constantly begging to charge across the street to get her. And all this before eight in the morning. Though, I was just as guilty… I hardly needed encouragement to hold Georgie in my mind after the previous night, I had woken up thinking of her. She practically infiltrated my dreams.

"She said anytime, Daddy," Kadee implored.

"Patience honey, if you don't finish your breakfast you won't be going at all."

Kadee pouted and pushed her eggs around the plate. I returned to my laptop hunting through the realtor listings as I had every morning since my offer across the street had fallen through. I noted two new listings, properties that might prove promising for a full-on restoration. The first of them was one town over but a fairly easy commute. I'd take a look at that one first and planned to call the agency promptly when the offices opened. I checked my watch, it was almost time.

"When you've finished your breakfast, do you think you can run into the garage and get your cycling pads? Daddy just needs to make a call."

"Yes!" squealed Kadee. She made short work of what remained of her breakfast, devouring the eggs mercilessly with the promise of a morning of fun to come.

"I'll be done here in a moment and we can go and she if Georgie's up."

I felt a little odd that Kadee was the excuse for me to head over and see Georgie this morning, like I was using my daughter as a prop so I could get a glimpse of the woman who'd dominated my thoughts and who'd managed to shake the cobwebs free from my heart. But then again Georgie had technically ruined Kadee's lesson yesterday, so it was only fair that she would make up for it, I thought playfully. That was all. I kept telling myself it would have nothing to do with what had happened between us, or the desperate urge I had to address the elephant stomping around the room of my head, begging me to take notice.

Without another word Kadee leapt from her stool and dashed off to the garage.

Checking my watch once again I made my calls. There was no reply at the first office and the second agent I tried, resulted in them needing to call me back. I flung my phone on the table and shut the laptop. The sense of urgency to find another house in order to fulfil my plans was mounting. But all thoughts of renovations, and flipping houses were obliterated when I heard a sudden crash from the garage.

"Kadee!" I called out in panic. I ran into the garage, my heart racing. Kadee stood there, a sheepish downcast look on her face. But from a quick glance at her, my eyes searching for a broken bone or a trickle of blood, I found she was unharmed. Thank god. The last thing I needed was Karen to accuse me of not taking care of Kadee properly.

At Kadee's feet a tool box lay on its side. It had been knocked off the workbench and its contents were strewn across the garage floor. Among the clutter with her pads half on awkwardly, Kadee finally lifted her eyes to mine, full of guilt.

"So sorry Daddy, my arm caught it," she said as her bottom lip trembled.

"That's okay, sweetie," I said, kneeling to collect up some of the tools. "It was only an accident." I stopped my task of putting things back in order when my daughter's face crumpled. I scooped her into my arms and felt a momentary shudder as she let out a quiet sob.

"Don't cry, baby girl. You did nothing wrong."

I pulled away to look at her. It was my fault. I had meant for Kadee to come and get changed in the house where I could see, I guess I still needed some practice in my directions.

"But aren't you going to yell at me? Are you going to send me home?"

I shook my head. "No, of course not. Why on earth would you think that?"

Kadee sniffed and used the back of her hand to rub at her button nose. I could see the uncertainty in my daughter's eyes and it troubled me.

"Kadee, you can tell me."

Her little shoulders juddered as she shrugged. "Brian doesn't like it when I make a mess."

I frowned at this admission and fought the immediate desire to succumb to my anger; thinking the worst of my ex-wife's new husband. Breathing through my nose, and taking great care with my tone, I asked, "Does Brian shout at you a lot?"

"Only when I've been naughty, or if I leave my toys out, or when I don't finish my meals, or if I'm too noisy… He makes me go to my room all the time."

So a lot then, I thought, biting my tongue. What else had my daughter had to put up with? From an outsider's perspective, Karen and Brian barely paid attention to her, yet still loved to use her as a pawn when dealing with me.

I gave her another hug, and wished everything had gone according to plan. If only I had the money to move out west to be closer to my daughter; if only I had won the bid for the house across the street. Now it felt like I was five steps behind, and precious time with my daughter was slipping through my fingers. She was growing up so fast. I needed to flip just one more house, then I'd have enough to afford a semi-decent place close-by to my ex from the sale of both properties. They lived in the city, brushing shoulders with celebs, and a house like this close-by with my budget would still be a forty minute drive. But it would be better than a costly six hour flight all the time.

"Don't worry, Daddy will fix this. I'm not going to shout at you and I'll make sure Brian knows he'll have me to deal with if he yells at you again."

"Okay," she replied with little conviction.

I adjusted the pads for her, made sure they were on nice and secure. Nothing bad was ever going to happen to my baby girl. I booped her on the nose for good measure, and returned the smile I managed to coax out of her.

"There we go, all tidy. Good as new, like nothing even happened. Now, shall we go and see Georgie?"

"Yes, yes," Kadee squeaked hopping on the spot, her smile broader than ever now.

I retrieved the bike from the garage and wheeled it for her as we crossed the road.

"What do you have to watch out for, Kadee?" I asked as we approached the porch.

"The bad steps," Kadee replied with slow rehearsed words.

"Smart cookie."

Kadee grabbed the porch banister and tip toed up the far right of the steps before leaping up to knock. A small indistinct shout came from inside and when I arrived to stand next to Kadee the door swung open.

Georgie had a coffee cup in one hand, the edge of the door in the other. Her hair was slightly disheveled, her face dreamy, and she blinked in the bright direct sunlight.

"Morning, late night?" I asked coyly, taking in her radiant glow. Fingers itching to feel the warmth of her sleepy body once again.

"Hey you," she returned matching my soft romantic tone, "and what's this you've brought me, it looks like a big pillow monster? Should I be scared?"

Kadee giggled and threw up her arms. "It's me, Georgie!"

"Aha, just the little lady I was thinking about. We are bike riding today aren't we?"

"Uh huh," nodded Kadee.

"Sorry if we're a little early. Did you sleep okay? I mean, we can come back if you're busy…" I said.

"No you're fine. Hey, I don't look that bad do I?" she said as she messed with her hair.

"Oh, no. Of course not. I didn't mean—"

Georgie laughed and bent down to inspect Kadee's pads. "Your dad gets a little tongue tied doesn't he?"

"It's probably cause he likes you," Kadee said, surprising us both.

"Kadee!" I blurted. "I…" I couldn't find the words and I

certainly couldn't deny the truth she'd let out into the world, not when Georgie was standing right there.

"You should quit while you're ahead. Besides I had the best night sleep since I got here," she said flashing me a sly wink. "Come on then, little monster let's get started."

"I'm not a monster," Kadee complained.

We strolled back across the street to get set up. Kadee was asking questions the whole time about how fast she would go and how long it would take her to cycle here from Mommy's. Georgie waited at one end of the drive watching us set off. She offered support to Kadee about shifting her weight and looking ahead, a pleasant change from the argument yesterday. Kadee kept peddling back and forth, her large pads rattling against the frame of the bike as she wobbled slowly forward.

From inside the house my phone rang and I was reminded of the urgency with the properties I needed to see.

"Shit, I need to get that!" I called out to Georgie, "do you think you could supervise for a moment?"

"Daddy!" exclaimed Kadee, pure shock evident on her young face. "You said a bad word."

I was confused for a moment till I realized the curse word I had let slip.

"Sorry!" I replied with a whine. I looked up to Georgie for acknowledgment as the phone continued to ring.

"Go. Us girls have got this. We don't need any stinky boys do we, Kadee?" she said and pulled a face, tongue out, eye crossed. Kadee wailed with laughter and I knew she was in good hands, as I rushed inside for the phone.

CHAPTER 12

Georgie

I turned the bike around for Kadee ready to take on another length of the driveway. Derek had disappeared into the house, he'd seemed fairly agitated and distracted by the call. But now here we were, me and Kadee. Maybe this was a good chance to make a decent impression. I wanted to make a difference in this cycling venture, it would obviously mean a great deal to Derek.

"How would you like to really impress your dad with your riding, Kadee?"

"Yes, please."

"Okay, here's what we need to do." I helped her off the bike carefully and wheeled it back toward the garage. "Your daddy is going to be so happy and proud of you. Now all we have to do is take off those awkward pads. They're only getting in the way and throwing off your balance."

As Kadee gratefully peeled off her over the top projection,

I set about removing one of the quick release training wheels. Kadee looked nervously back at the house.

"Are you sure this is okay, Georgie?"

"You're perfect with just the helmet and gloves, I promise. This is how I learned," I reassured her.

She studied me for a moment and then gave a single nod.

"Now, you only have a training wheel on the left so if you feel yourself falling over this way," I said as I waved over to my house, "you lean back toward your house, to regain your balance okay? Keep the handle bars nice and straight."

Kadee nodded again thoughtfully and agreed. Then clambered back on, raring to give it a go, as I held the bike steady.

"Now if you think your going to fall, you just get to high five the ground right. Well perhaps a low five." I held out my palm flat for Kadee to hit it.

"High five!" she said, slapping my palm.

"That's it girl." I stepped back a few feet from the bike. "Now I want you to peddle to me."

With a look of absolute concentration she wobbled forward, pausing to lean at times. I took another small step backward as she advanced.

"There we go, you're doing great. You're an absolute natural!"

Kadee's grin broadened as she wobbled forward just a little faster. After a couple of lengths of the driveway her confidence was growing quickly. She no longer needed any help turning the bike around and remounting, I only needed to stand by, offering encouragement.

"What we can do soon is switch over the training wheels to practice the other side," I explained as she make ready for another length.

We had just set off again when Derek appeared from the house, with one look he called out loudly.

"Kadee, what are you doing?" He rushed across the lawn to us.

"Look Daddy, it's easy!" Kadee shouted as she accelerated.

"What on earth are you playing at?" Derek directed at me as he drew near. I halted in my steps taken back by his tone. "I step away for a moment and you—"

"Just wait. Trust me," I said, keeping my eyes on Kadee. "She's doing great, look," I added in my defence, gesturing to Kadee who was advancing quickly along the driveway.

Derek was still moving after her, but with a little less urgency than he had at first. He watched her as he slowed.

"See Daddy, can you see?" she yelled from up ahead.

"Yes, baby. You look great. But be careful."

As if his words had tempted fate Kadee's front wheel snagged on a small divot causing the handlebars to angle to the side and she tumbled onto the driveway. She landed with a small squeal, slapping her palms down to steady her fall. Just liked I'd shown her.

"Kadee!" Derek screamed, launching off after her again. I half wanted to hold him back, but he was already gone when I reached out.

Luckily however, by the time he arrived by her side she had already straightened the bike and was almost back on.

"Are you okay? Are you hurt? Kadee, sweetie?" he asked kneeling beside her, checking over inch of her little body.

"I'm okay. It was just a low five," she said to his bewilderment. "I think I bumped my elbow though."

"Let me see."

Kadee held up her elbow for him to inspect.

"Oh well, that's just a little boo boo. You're such a brave girl. I'll go get a plaster—"

"No, Daddy, it's just a boo boo," Kadee reiterated adorably. "Kiss it better instead."

Like any dutiful father he followed his daughter's instruction and kissed her elbow sweetly.

"Daddy can we switch the training wheels now?"

"I suppose we could. You look like you're getting the hang of it."

"Georgie is a good teacher."

"Yeah... seems she is good at a lot of things," agreed Derek looking up at me. His tone warm and endearing again.

"Maybe we should take her out to dinner, to thank her. Shouldn't we?"

"Erm, what?" Derek hesitated, with this out of the blue suggestion, "Well, we don't know if she's busy honey. Georgie has a life of her own you know?"

I stood there amused as his little devious and yet totally adorable child threw him on the spot. Practically playing matchmaker. Then I butted into the conversation to rescue him... or add fuel to the flames, depending on your perspective.

"I'm not busy, I was taking the day off anyway. I really need to recharge after the move."

"So you'll come to dinner with us, Georgie?" Kadee asked, hands already on the handlebars raring to go again.

"Only if your dad—"

"Come out with us tonight?" he said, meeting my smile, his tone had a decisive edge to it, and I couldn't help but glow from the inside out from what this could mean. "There is a new place in town we could try."

"I would love to."

"Though of course you'll get the two of us again," he added, gesturing to himself and Kadee.

"A package deal? Well that's even better. How could I resist?"

"Yay!" came Kadee's squeal and we both laughed as she peddled off up the driveway.

CHAPTER 13

Derek

"So what is this place?" Georgie asked from the passenger seat.

We were taking my truck into town. Kadee sat in the back quietly watching the buildings go by as we drove down Main street.

"Nothing fancy I'm afraid, a good old family restaurant as far as I'm aware. The owner is an old friend of my dad's actually."

"Small town, huh?"

"Yeah. I've heard good things about the food. Maybe as good as your mac and cheese."

She laughed. "Hey that's just the tip of the iceberg, I'm a great cook! I just need a functioning kitchen."

"We'll have to see about that then."

"About what, my cooking or my kitchen? I think it's best to keep you out of there… it'll only lead to trouble."

"I will, if you promise to stop dropping things." We threw each other a mischievous smile.

"Are we there yet?" chimed in Kadee from the back.

"As a matter of fact we are. I hope you're hungry sweetie," I answered, finding a parking space a couple of cars down from the restaurant.

I helped Kadee out of the back, and almost immediately once her feet touched the ground she darted to Georgie's side, and took her hand. Georgie gave my little girl the most heartwarming smile. She caught me watching and shrugged as if it was nothing... but it wasn't nothing. Her and Kadee getting along so well was a weird dream come true. I'd hadn't planned on being with anyone, it had never really been on the agenda while I'd been so focused on flipping houses, and it never occurred to me either while Kadee was around. But this, the three of us, together, was something really good.

"You look gorgeous by the way," I offered to Georgie as we headed along the sidewalk. It had felt a little odd meeting up at my driveway earlier and I had been too busy helping Kadee to offer any remark on how good she looked. But now seeing her in the glow of the soft light that spilled from the restaurant I couldn't hold my tongue any longer.

"This old thing? You're the one looking fancy, you scrub up pretty well yourself for a man that seems to live in jeans," she replied with a glint in her eye. Her cheeks had darkened slightly and I couldn't help but think that her response was a defence mechanism. I made a mental note to tell her more often how beautiful she was, how even the slightest quirk of her lips made my heart race. And how, for some reason, I could barely remember a time before she'd walked into my—our—lives.

Opening the door for my ladies, the atmosphere that met us inside was somewhere between homely and romantic. Warm red furnishing adorned the place, light sparkled from the wall fittings and candles in tea-light holders. Classic old world photos adorned the walls in ornate frames. I approached the empty pedestal by the entrance as a busy waiter rushed past with two plates in hand.

"I'll be there in a moment folks," he called back.

The restaurant was surprisingly busy for midweek. Happy chatter bubbled over the place from the numerous occupied tables.

"I have a table under Varden," I told him when the waiter returned.

"Ah, the Vardens, glad you could join us this evening," he announced cheerfully, "this way please, we have your table ready."

I had little chance to correct his obvious presumption that we were all the Varden family. I turned to shrug at Georgie as we followed him, she smiled and led Kadee through the tables.

We were seated in a nice quiet corner, and I settled down with a warm sense of happiness, despite the nerves accumulating in my belly from the date I'd suddenly found myself taking part in. It'd been years since I'd been out with anyone, and certainly never with Kadee acting as a chaperone. But I needn't have worried. Georgie was helping Kadee with her menu and the two of them had not stopped talking since she had got out of the car. I had a pang of sadness at how much I missed this togetherness. Kadee's bright smile made everything a delight, and Georgie's happy features had an even greater effect on me. She looked even more beautiful in the candle light.

We were finishing up our main course when a deep booming voice carried over the table.

"Ah there he is. Derek, how are you doing?" It was the owner Bernard, or Bernie as folks called him.

I half stood to welcome him and shake the hand he had

proffered, "Hey Bernie. It's been a while, great place you have here. It's about time we came and saw it."

"Thank you, thank you, my boy. Heck I haven't seen you for nearly a decade."

"Guess so, I heard you'd left town?"

"Yes, yes, my big plans. I opened up a place in the city. Thought I was going to make it big. Turns out this is what my heart really needed," he waved his arms around him at the surroundings and occupied tables. "A local, family place. Each customer a familiar face."

"Good to have you back, I have to say. The place is just great."

"And the food is delicious," Georgie interjected.

"Thank you, but not too many compliments to the chef please, they tend to get a big head and soon enough Simon will want a raise," Bernie chuckled. "However these two lovely ladies deserve all the compliments this evening. You're a lucky man, Derek."

"That I am. Sorry, where are my manners? This is Georgie, my…" I trailed off, unable to define our relationship. What were we? We hadn't nailed anything down and I didn't want to presume.

"His friend," Georgie said rescuing me from embarrassment. Though that was quickly short-lived.

"His girlfriend," Kadee added with a giggle.

A quick look at Georgie and I found although she was biting her lip, she didn't seem to mind the new title bestowed upon her.

"And this is my darling daughter, Kadee."

"Pleased to meet you all. Derek you have a lovely evening with such delightful ladies. I will let you all get on with your meal, and if there's anything you need you only have to ask."

Bernie bowed and took his leave.

With our main course cleared it was time to debate

dessert. The debate however was rather short lived when Kadee spotted a chocolate gateaux being delivered to another table nearby. Thought she did describe it at "ga-tux" and a few hilarious minutes followed as we practiced the proper pronunciation with her. Georgie sounded rather sexy as she surprisingly fell into a fake French accent with ease.

"Don't look at me like that," she said laughing.

"Like what?"

"So I took some classes," Georgie said with a wave of her hand and spent some time in France.

"That certainly paid off, *ma chérie*," I said and caught her hand, meeting her eyes. We stared at each other, lost for a second as the noises from the restaurant melted away. But then she blinked and reclaimed her hand, placing it back in her lap. I wasn't the only one nervous tonight…

"I don't think I could eat a whole portion though. I could get a kid's one like Kadee, unless you want to share?" said Georgie.

"Yeah, that sounds perfect. I'm pretty full too."

I shuffled my seat round closer to Georgie as the dessert arrived and she slid it over between us. Kadee was happily tucking in, though I had a feeling there would need to be some sort of napkin intervention required when she was finished. More of the cake seemed to make it onto her cheeks than in her mouth.

Georgie started in on our portion, and she gave out a moan of appreciation at the first spoonful.

"That good huh?" I inquired.

"Mmm, you should try this," she said as another spoonful found her mouth.

"If I get a chance," I joked, I covered her hand with mine again, this time not letting her get away so fast, as she went back for more.

She paused as our warm hands rested on top of each

other on the table. There was that electricity again, our eyes met longingly for an endless moment. I so badly wanted to kiss her, to lean over like it was an everyday occurrence. Instead my nerves got the best of me, I didn't think I was ready for it to be real, or to kiss someone in front of my daughter. Not when I didn't have it all figured out yet. Because this wasn't in my plans. Georgie coming along when she had, had thrown a spanner in the works in more ways than one.

"If you're not careful I'm going to bite your hand so I can get more cake."

I tsked with a teasing smile. "Do you not have any table manners?"

Quickly, I wrestled the spoon from her distracted grip. She pouted and stuck her chocolaty tongue out at me then turned to Kadee.

"Do you like it Kadee?" she asked.

"It's yummy! I want more!"

Using Georgie's spoon I scooped up a bit of cake.

"That better be for me," Georgie giggled then gasped when I stole a bite.

"Nope, all mine," I declared, keeping my eyes locked on hers.

It was all so heart warming, and it pained me think of the disastrous plans with the house that had fallen through and how my time together with Kadee and Georgie was slipping away. Soon enough Karen would want Kadee to go back to her, and I would follow too if I kept to my plans. I needed to be close to my daughter. I needed to see her grow up. That was no longer negotiable. But that would also mean leaving Georgie behind.

There couldn't be many more nights like this however much I wanted it. Or Georgie.

CHAPTER 14

Georgie

I was in a dreamy mood as Derek drove us home, it had been such a great night, a wonderful atmosphere surrounded by good people. I began to feel hopeful about the little town I'd decided to plant my roots. And as if to prove the point, Bernie's farewells when we'd finished at the restaurant were accompanied with big friendly hugs, calling out that he couldn't wait to see us all again.

Kadee was such a joy, so well behaved and funny, and she was only overshadowed by Derek's eyes, his looks of longing. It had felt so right with the three of us together despite the short time I had known them both. It was like we were already becoming a close-knit unit, and I was very sure I didn't want the night to end. Though I didn't think asking to come in for coffee was appropriate in front of Kadee, so I bit my tongue.

"How about a movie?" Derek asked me to my relief and delight when we got out of the truck. "What do you say Kadee?"

"Yes, please stay, Georgie," Kadee implored.

"I'd love to honey."

Derek offered me an arm for support as I made my way over the stepping stones on the lawn in my heels, then kicked them off once we got inside. Derek instructed Kadee to get changed into her pyjamas before we could watch the movie.

"Come see my room, Georgie!"

"I'll give her a hand," I offered, heading upstairs with her as Derek got busy tidying up a little, shifting some paper work and his laptop from the coffee table.

When we returned downstairs Kadee dragged me to the sofa.

"Can I get you a drink?" Derek offered as he headed into the kitchen.

"Hmm what have you got?"

"Well, actually only beer. Or coffee…"

"Beer is fine with me." I had only had a small glass of wine at dinner, I would happily have another drink.

He returned with two nice cold ones and settled into the sofa as well. Kadee leaned into him as she sat between us. He ruffled her hair lovingly.

"Question is what do we want to watch, cause I'm easy."

"Oh really?" I immediately said followed by a mischievous glance at him.

"Nemo!" Kadee squealed out as Derek flicked through the options.

Pausing he looked over to me, seemingly for my opinion. "Just keep swimming!" He frowned at my response and Kadee wiggled pretending to be a fish. "Sure, I've always loved it, I'm sold," I added for clarity.

We all snuggled down to the movie and listened to

Kadee's giggles. She got steadily sleepier and before we were halfway through she was sound asleep, her head resting on my lap, her feet pressed up against Derek's thigh.

"I'd better get her to bed," Derek said, scooping up the sleeping darling.

"Need any help?"

"No you stay, I won't be a moment."

My mind wandered as the movie continued while Derek was upstairs. He was the perfect father, maybe a little over protective but he had a such a sweet endearing quality to him that made my insides yearn, an ache for this simple, yet charming life he led. I wanted to be apart of it.

Biting my lip, unable to stop my train of thought, I wondered if maybe I would be scooped up next.

A second later I dismissed the wayward thought. I was getting ahead of myself. Involving myself with a single-dad had not been what I came here for. I was supposed to be taking care of myself not falling head over heels in…

Distracting myself, I got up with the sense that the night was over and looked around the immaculate room. The interior was all crafted beautifully, but on further inspection it was all a little bare. There was no real color or personal character to the place. Where were all the soft-furnishings, the art on the wall, the little nicknacks? It needed a woman's touch to become a proper home, maybe more kids toys too. I shook my head again. Wanting the thoughts to stop, but not having the heart to completely push them away. And then the thought I'd spun around in my mind became more literal. Would Derek like a woman's touch tonight? My touch…

As I strolled the room I glanced over the papers that he had shifted to the sideboard. There were some letters regarding mortgages and a stack of listings printed out. It seemed rather private, but I glanced through houses with curiosity, I couldn't resist looking at great houses. I just caught the street name on the last one when I heard Derek heading downstairs. Quickly, as if I'd been caught robbing a bank, I dropped the papers back where I found them.

That was our street. Chestnut Grove. Why was he looking at houses on our street? The only house that had been put up for sale recently, as far as the agent had told me, was mine.

"I should probably get going, I have plans early tomorrow," I said as he came into view.

"Really? But—" he replied not finishing, unsuccessfully masking the disappointment in his voice. He stepped toward me where I stood beside the sofa.

"It was a pretty great night though, thank you. We should do it again. It was lovely being with you two. All three of us…"

"It may not be that easy," he said with a hint of sadness.

Puzzled, I was about to question him, when his arms slid around me and I was again held in his divine embrace. Our lips met slowly. Tentatively finding their groove. Oh, who was I kidding? I wasn't going anywhere. But before my body and mind was completely lost to him, two considerations demanded my attention.

"What about Kadee?" I hesitated, breaking the kiss for a second.

"Fast asleep. She sleeps like a rock. But just in case, we can be quiet can't we?" he said, pinching my bum as a taunt.

"Depends on what you do to me. I can't promise anything, but I can try," I said batting my lashes. "We better be safe this time, too."

"You're perfectly safe with me, Georgie," he replied and stopped me from stalling anymore. I slid my arms around his neck and dove back into the pool of desire.

CHAPTER 15

Derek

I didn't want to let her leave, it had been such a perfect night. It couldn't be over that soon. I wanted her here with me.

I had to forget the troubles that was going on—they could wait for daylight. She was all that mattered right now. Her warm lips had never felt so good, I held her tightly and caressed her body through the elegant little black dress she wore. Her tongue teased at mine and I wrestled it back, kissing her deeper, making her breathe that little bit harder. Loving the feel of her billowing chest, battling for air, against my body.

My hungry hands squeezed her sexy ass and tugged her dress up over it. She sat herself up on the arm of the sofa and I eased up to her sliding my hands all the way back up into her hair, looking deep into her eyes before kissing her achingly slowly. She was unbuttoning my shirt all the while.

After the final button her teasing fingers traced downward over my chest and stomach. I threw off the shirt to let her fingers roam freely.

With my arms around her again I unzipped her dress. She was busy tugging at my belt and waist buttons. Slipping the back of her dress open I ran my hands over the smooth bare skin. Nothing had ever felt so good. She arched slightly and I lent into her more to plant my lips on her neck.

Georgie murmured as I kissed and nibbled her gently, and sank her hands into my opened trousers to feel for me. She pulled my rapidly hardening cock up and out of its confines, holding and stroking it with the same gentleness I applied to her sensual neck. Her touch was heavenly and the firmer I nibbled into her neck the harder she stroked and played.

"Let's head upstairs," I said as things escalated.

"Lead the way," she purred back at me, still stroking and watching me with those seductive eyes.

Quietly I led her by the hand upstairs to the bedroom, and carefully closed the door. I adjusted the dimmer on the light and sat on the bed to discard my pants, shorts and socks. I opened the bedside table draw to claim protection from an unopened box and placed it on the table ready. When I sat there naked Georgie slowly slipped out of her dress letting it fall to the floor. Admiring her body, I watched her. My pulse pounding for her to come closer.

In her matching lacy underwear she approached me, and I could've sworn she was the most beautiful woman I'd ever seen. I was in awe of her. She straddled my lap where I sat and draped her arms around my neck.

"You're such a goddess," I whispered as my hands began to roam her body, revelling in how smooth and good she felt under my touch.

"And you... you're too damn sexy and you don't even

know it," she whispered in return hugging my neck a little tighter.

"I could say the same to you. You have no idea. The first moment I saw you, fuck I needed you."

She met my lips again as I continued to caress her, along her thighs, up and down her back, then up her front to tease her soft full breasts beneath her bra. She sighed against my lips. In response I tugged at the prison and freed the two round captives, and took my time to give them the attention they deserved.

I leaned in to kiss them lovingly while she played her fingers through my hair. Soft gentle kisses I planted all over her, before teasing her nipples with the firm tip of my tongue. My tongue swam over her buds until they stood up in appreciation. She unfastened her bra and threw it aside. Smoothing my hands over her body again I met her fully exposed breasts and squeezed firmly. Pinching her nipples as I massaged her warm yielding flesh. She bit her lip and wriggled closer against me, my now rock hard cock between us as it pressed at her knickers. I pulsed, begging to be let past the barrier.

Her breasts fell softly against my chest as I slid my hands down to hold and fondle her ass, tugging on her cheeks as she wriggled against me, teasing me till I found it hard to keep my eyes open.

"Woman you're driving me insane," I said with a hiss, as she continued to grind her pelvis, brushing her sweet pussy against the head of my cock. The friction was almost unbearable.

After another deep longing stare into her eyes I suddenly spun her from my lap and flung her onto her back on the bed. She gave out a small squeak of shock and lay there with a mischievous smile.

"I thought you wanted to be quiet?"

"I never said silent."

I moved up beside her supporting myself on one elbow and found her lips again. Tasting a hint of sweet chocolate and malty beer. Deep and passionately we kissed as I slid my other hand smoothly down between her legs. My fingers coasted under her knickers, she felt so good to my touch, hot, wet, and welcoming. I eased them inside her as she took a breath, body curving. She sighed quietly as my bowed finger got to work. I worked her firmly and steadily for a good while, letting my cock regain its focus, kissing her now and again as her moans increased, barely a breath between each one.

But despite trying to slow things down, Georgie reached for my cock, this time with greater urgency. In her tight slow grip she almost made me lose my rhythm.

No longer able to resist, I moved to tug her knickers off, then slipping on the condom I was upon her again. She spread her legs eagerly to welcome me and I hovered close to her, the tip of my cock touching her wet lips.

"I want you so much," she whispered, her tingling nails tracing over my chest.

"I'm right here," I replied.

"You better not break my heart," she said against my ear as she pulled me down toward her. Not knowing what to say, I decided to respond and show her exactly what I was feeling instead.

Slowly I eased myself inside her, parting her lips, plunging inch by inch. She threw her arms around me lovingly as I started to thrust. So slow at first yet hard and deep I rocked her. Our quiet, intense breathing grew heavier with each deep push. I watched her questioning eyes and licked at her tongue, our breathless mouths open. She squirmed beneath me as the steady pace continued, the intense desire in her eyes growing ever more fierce.

She was biting her lip hard between quiet panting, her pleasure arousing me beyond words. The urge to explode rising like a tidal wave.

When a louder moan half escaped her lips I slowed and for a second covered her mouth with my hand. She rolled her eyes, smirked then nibbled on my finger, taking it into her hot mouth. I let her suck before I spun us over till she was straddled on top of me. She sat up and with her hands gripping my chest started to grind herself on me. It my turn to break the silence, groaning as she writhed.

Her pussy hugged me tightly as she rocked on top. She flung her head back, working up a fast and effortless motion. Bouncing slightly on my cock, her body bobbing up and down giving me a sight that almost made me lose control. A front row seat to the greatest show on earth.

Trying to hold on, I wanted this to last. Slowing the pace I gripped her hips, watching her magnificence breasts wiggle with the easy rhythm we'd found. Catching her glance I nodded to her, she flung her head back again and ground against me harder and slower. Her nails were digging into my chest, her thighs squeezing around me. I tensed beneath her and she eased up, almost releasing my primed cock only to drive back down onto me forcing me so deep inside her cunt.

She went through this motion several more time, harder and deeper, until, using my cock like a fireman's pole. Up and down, up and down. My eyelids slamming shut, toes clenched… unable to bear another second. As her ass cheeks slapped against my thighs once more, I burst deep inside her. She gasped silently and I took over, thrusting as her senses overloaded. Georgie fell down onto me, her body almost collapsing like a demolished building. I embraced her, not letting her fall just yet, and thrust my pelvis hard again, hammering my still throbbing cock into her until she in turn tensed up and came.

When our waves of pleasure began to subside, the dust finally settling, and our breathing eased she slumped to my side snuggling against me stroking my chest to survey the damage.

"Oh my god," she murmured.

"Agreed, that was glorious," I replied, "you are glorious," I corrected. "Who knew being so quiet could be so hot."

She smiled and kissed me softly. "And who knew I was going to have such a hot neighbor," she said.

"Yeah?" I said a little half heartedly, as all my thoughts of the house plans swelled up again.

For a moment, we allowed our breathing to slow, each battling with the silence of the room.

"Derek. What's wrong?"

"Nothing, it's fine."

"Tell me... Did I do something wrong?"

"No," I replied, partly lying, never wanting to reveal the truth on how she'd stolen my dream away from me. Because in its place, another dream had arose.

"Then what is it? Is it what you told me the other day? About moving? I thought you loved it here, don't you?"

I sighed. "I do, it's just Kadee. I keep trying to put a plan together to be with her and every time it's like I take one step forward but two back."

"So you would move to be with her?"

"In a heartbeat, wouldn't you move to be with the one you love?"

"I guess I would," she said thoughtfully. She sat up and with a more defiant tone added. "I can't believe you don't get to see her more. Sounds like the worst custody agreement ever."

"Well, we never sorted anything like that. Karen just up

and moved. Wanted to follow her acting career. Then she met that douchebag… It's not like I can have a say now Kadee lives all the way across the country."

"That's nonsense, you're her father," Georgie said as she took my hand. "You have rights. Hell, I'm meeting my friend tomorrow in the city. I may not really know what I'm talking about when it comes to this sort of thing, but she'll have a good idea of what you could do. She's a lawyer. Maybe I could ask her?"

"I don't know…" The last thing I wanted was to get Georgie involved in my mess, but maybe this was a sign. I also didn't want to think of the potential disastrous ramifications getting a lawyer would have on the situation, what if Karen actually won? And I never got to see Kadee ever again? But Georgie made it sound promising. "You think it would help?"

"I'm sure it would. You have to at least try, right? How about I come over tomorrow evening and we can talk more about it?"

"Sure, so you're away all day?"

"Why, are you going to miss me?" She snuggled back into my arms.

"Maybe," I replied coyly and kissed the top of her head.

CHAPTER 16

Georgie

It was early, and I was driving into the city to meet Fiona for lunch. I glanced over to Derek's, the house still looked all quiet. Before dawn I'd managed to sneak out without waking him or Kadee and hurried back over to my own bed. And surprisingly, the walk of shame wasn't all that shameful. The whole night had been heart-thumpingly good. Especially the tail end, in his bed, our hands and bodies yearning to be close again. God, I could've fucked him all day—from morning noon and night—rubbing myself raw on his cock.

It was undeniable how much I longed to see him again already. Later, I told myself, envisaging sneaking over to him after my jaunt in the city. I couldn't let Fiona down, I'd already blown off several of her lunch date requests. So with a slight sigh and a pang of regret, I jumped in my truck and set off.

Seeing Fiona was probably the best thing to do right now anyway. I needed an outsiders perspective, I needed her to tell me I was fucking crazy for getting involved with a single-dad who obviously had problems of his own, not to mention the added baggage of his ex. Kadee however, was far from baggage… she was a cute little accessory, adorable in every way. But was I ready to become so involved in their lives… in her life? That was a huge responsibility. And no doubt, dating Derek meant knowing she was part of the deal too.

Could I be a stepmom?

The thought zapped me from out of nowhere. See, this was why I needed Fiona, I was already travelling faster than light, letting my brain off the leash. Being a stepmom would mean marriage, and hell, we'd only known each other not that long! Fiona needed to tell me to slow my roll.

Fiona met me outside the restaurant with a cheery greeting and hug.

"Well, someone looks bright and breezy this morning. You're all glowy and shit."

"Hey, lunch with my BFF, of course I am."

She looked me over quizzically when we were sat, menus in hand.

"I call bullshit. No, something's definitely up with you. You never smile this much… unless." She paused for effect. "You've been getting some! Haven't you? Back on the horse are you? Tell me, tell me. Which cowboy are you riding now?"

I glanced around, nervous at the volume of her voice and tried to shh her.

"Don't you shh me," she said giggling. "Oh, don't tell me, I know who it is. The hunky neighbor, right? Well played. It was the faded Levis that did it, wasn't it? And all those bulging muscles… one in particular I bet. So, spill the beans."

"God you are incorrigible," I hissed. "And just because I

happen to have a healthy glow, doesn't automatically mean I'm getting fucked five ways from Sunday."

"But you so are, you dirty little hussy! Details, now."

"Oh a lady never tells."

"Good thing you aren't a lady then."

I rolled my eyes. "Fine, I got some. Happy now?"

"Not yet but I will be once you tell me more.

"But I'm not sure what there is to tell."

"You don't get off that easy. If there's nothing to tell, why are you glowing, you're practically on fire! Like damn, I want some of what she's having!" Fiona said pretending to flag down a waiter.

"Okay god. Are you determined to let everyone in the restaurant know that I got laid? Fine," I said again, resigning myself to her interrogation. "I don't really know, it all just sort of happened. I think it was gonna be this one night thing but then yesterday... We had a great day together, and then..."

"And then you had another great night?" Fiona butted in.

"Yes, a great night too. Maybe too great. God he did this thing, and Fiona... oh my god, I nearly screamed the house down. But I had to keep quiet cause you know, he had a daughter who's staying with him right now. Then I kinda had to sneak out this morning, I couldn't stay. Kadee might not be ready for seeing me coming out of her dad's bedroom, and Derek and I haven't really discussed it. Hadn't had the chance." Noticing Fiona's furrowed brow I quickly added, "His daughter, she's five. Cute as a button and he's very protective of her."

Fiona nodded knowingly. "Ah, single dad. I think my little Georgie's falling hard here, and maybe not just for him, huh?"

"It's not so simple."

"Is anything?"

"I just don't know what's happening. We started this thing, and it's amazing, but I can't fall for him."

"Why ever not?"

"I think he's planning on moving. And I don't mean just around the block. He's in a real mess with his daughter. She lives out west and I think he's going to leave soon so he can be a proper dad, you know full-time."

"Have you asked him?" asked Fiona bluntly.

"Well no, there's a lot going on, what with the house as well."

"Sure, I know. And you've been a little busy jumping his bones," Fiona joked lightly. "If only there was a simple way you could find out what's going on." She stroked her chin, impersonating a thoughtful scientist or thinker. "You know, like fucking asking him! You like him don't you, so just ask him already. Don't beat around the bush. Life's too short for that bullshit."

"Maybe," I replied hesitantly.

"No maybe, go for it girl!"

"God, I hate it when you're right."

Lifted by her confidence and straight forwardness I shrugged and nodded my half agreement.

"Meanwhile, how's the house going?" she continued.

"Ergh, don't ask. I don't seem to be getting anywhere. So much for my dream home. There's so much to do. But I'm determined to get it done. I'll turn the house into a home soon enough."

"Didn't you tell me this neighbor of yours was pretty handy? Sounds like you could be putting his hands to good use in more ways than one."

"No, Fiona. The whole point was I was doing this for myself. This was my dream. Put down roots, stand on my own two feet, and put the work in. I want to do it myself, it wouldn't be right if I gave up and suddenly got him to do the work while I sat back and twiddled my thumbs."

"Oh, I don't see the harm. What if he you worked on it with you, together? You can hang out and fix up your place. Kill two birds with one stone, nail him to the wall a few times… you know, let him inspect your carpeting."

I burst out laughing, my mind suddenly back to my very first night with Derek. We'd almost knocked down my bedroom wall.

"Did anyone ever tell you you have a filthy mind?"

"Only every time we see each other," Fiona said laughing. "I'm serious though, it's so much to take on by yourself. A little help never harmed anyone."

I considered this, and the prospect of hanging out with him and Kadee as we all worked on a project did sound like a heap of fun and a jolly good mess.

"I just don't want him taking control. He's totally the know-it all type, my way or the highway kinda guy when it comes to his profession, his passion. But maybe you're right-"

"Score two for me!"

I ignored her and continued my train of thought, "I could ask him to help out. I have been helping out with Kadee, god she's so sweet, and I could do more of that. A small trade. Actually, speaking of which I also wanted to talk to you about something that might give me an edge, what do you know about child custody agreements?"

"Hmm, family law, a little but not enough. I know a guy, why?"

"He never gets to see his daughter, and they are great together. She lives with her mom, in California and he's going to be heartbroken when she has to go home. Which will be soon from what I've gathered. Kadee is only here cause his ex got married and dumped the kid on him at the last minutes so she could go honeymooning."

Fiona frowned, "I can reach out for sure, this guy owes me anyhow."

"Thank you, you're a star."

"How about we fill our faces now. Look at this stuff," she said, brandishing the menu dramatically, then turned to find the nearest passing waiter. "Please bring us a couple of screwdrivers, a double for me, 'cause my friend can't be the only one getting laid," she said waggling her eyebrows.

CHAPTER 17

Derek

Knowing my mother—as well as my father—would kill me if they didn't get to spend some time with Kadee while she was here, I dropped Kadee off at my parent's house for some quality time.

My mom had a day of baking and gardening planned for them both and though Kadee hadn't really wanted to stay with them, once there was mention of cookies she changed her tune rather quickly. To be fair Kadee didn't know either of them that well so there was bound to be some nerves. But I had a job that I couldn't afford to miss out on despite Kadee's complaints on the drive there. However with the warm greeting and the promise of activities my mom had planned, had finally convinced her the stay was worthwhile. I hugged and kissed by baby girl goodbye, thanked my mom, and rushed off.

It was just my luck that while I was on route to the job,

that they called to cancel. Some other delays in the pipeline meant I wouldn't be needed for another week. I cursed and pondered my day again taking the turn back to my house.

I was happy to let Kadee have the time bonding with her gran and pop, and I knew it would mean the world to them both. And I couldn't help but wish it was always like this, Kadee with me, able to play in the garden, in the fresh air, with the chance to get to know my side of the family. Maybe even meet some of her cousins. But that was probably never going to happen, I thought, resigning myself that I would still need to move out west in order to see my baby girl more than once or twice a year.

Deciding to let my parents have their time with their youngest granddaughter, the thought of Georgie crossed my mind. Though in all honesty, I had not really stopped thinking of her. The memories of our times together seemed to ease my worries, making me hopeful. There was something about her that I craved and couldn't shake. Her stubborn attitude drove me insane and yet I wouldn't have her any other way.

I pulled into the drive thinking I would love to do something nice for Georgie while she was away, to show my affections for her, to say thank you for making me stop and enjoy the simple things, and not be so consumed by worry all the time. I glanced over at her empty house, an idea taking form. Maybe the greatest way for me to do that was with what I knew best. Nodding, I promptly jumped out the truck, retrieved my supplies from the garage, strapped on my tool belt, and got to work.

I was well under way tearing out the steps of the porch when my phone rang.

"Derek, hey, can you hear me? God this line is terrible."

"Karen?"

"Yeah, okay I have to be quick. We're cutting the honeymoon short. There's a hurricane on the way, we have to get out of here, fast."

"Are you serious?"

"So the only flight we could get lands us on the east coast tomorrow, but that works out so that we drive down to you and pick Kadee up before flying home."

"What? But I have another week with her."

"You don't if we are taking her home. I'm escaping from imminent danger here and you're worried about another week of babysitting?"

As ever, her blasé tone instantly irritated me. "I'm not babysitting. She's my god damn daughter!"

"Well I'm sure you've had a fine time hammering nails together, but it's all arranged. I'll let you know the times on the day. Listen I have to go, things are complete mayhem here."

Infuriated I slammed down the length of wood I still held in my other hand before I was tempted to smash it over something. As I stood, squeezing the life out of my mobile, I tried to absorb the news. I had always wanted Kadee in my life, but this past week had been so amazing it choked me up thinking of her leaving again so soon. We had already been making fun plans for next week, I couldn't bare to think of her face when I told her that we had to cancel.

There had to be a better way.

I threw myself back into the work as I struggled with my thoughts, what if I couldn't get my plan together and move out west? What about Georgie if I did? Getting custody of my little girl was a long shot and it felt like time was running out. Things felt such a mess when only yesterday it all felt like a wonderful dream.

I lost track of time and my progress on Georgie's porch steps was slow as my mind bounced from problem to problem, and typically as if echoing my mood, the weather turned and it started to rain heavily. Water washed over the porch and puddles began to form in the dirt I had exposed. It quickly began to look like an unpleasant swamp with rotten wood and mud all around.

Just marvelous. I wouldn't be able to set the concrete footings in this weather and the rain would set the work back for a few days. This was not going to be the best welcome home for Georgie.

"What the hell are you doing?" came the sudden loud challenge from behind me, followed by the slam of a car door.

I hadn't noticed Georgie driving up while I'd stood in the rain inspecting the half-finished job. But now she was here, she was advancing up her path with a bewildered and angry look on her face.

"Georgie, hey. I hadn't planned for things to look like this, I thought you'd be out longer."

"Oh I'm sorry, did you need more time to rip my house apart?"

"Wait just a second. This is going to be great when it's finished. And you know these steps are a hazard, I was only trying to help."

"Yes I'm very well aware of that. What do you think I have in the truck there? I bought supplies. I'm on this, I don't need you to intervene. What did you think, we sleep together and you have free reign over all my affairs? To think, I was trying to help you out today with Kadee, but that was only because you knew about it. I didn't go around your back."

"Maybe I don't need you interfering in my affairs either. Hell, if you hadn't thrown your money at this house, I'd be okay! Things were just great before you arrived!" I spat back, the accumulation of all my frustrations sharpening to a point, aimed directly at her.

Her angry brow furrowed once more. "What the fuck is that suppose to mean?"

"It means, you kind of ruined everything, okay? Like women always do!"

"I've had enough." She didn't want to hear another word, holding out her hand she stormed off furiously toward her back door. I didn't watch her leave this time, too angry to take the words back, and snatched up my tools and headed home instead.

Seriously, how come every time I tried to help out things turned bad? Was I best staying out of it? If Kadee was leaving again I knew I wanted to desperately turn my mind to my moving plans. I didn't even know how Georgie could fit into that... But I couldn't worry about Georgie, or how she blew everything out of proportion, right now. It was getting late and I needed to pick up Kadee. If tomorrow was going to be my last day with my daughter, every hour with her counted even more.

∽

"Daddy!"

My mom opened the door and Kadee rushed out into my waiting arms.

"Hey baby, how have you been? Did you have fun?"

"She's been a darling," mom replied.

"I like my new nana. She let me eat cookie dough, then I had two warm cookies, but we saved some for you, Georgie too."

"Well that's sweet, you wanted to share huh?"

"This Georgie sounds nice. Anything I should know about? I have been hearing about her all day. She sounds a darn sight better than, you know who." My mom's poorly veiled venom for my ex reared its ugly head as ever and I swallowed a groan.

With Kadee held in my arms I turned her away from my mother's sour tone, giving her a look aimed to curb any onslaught. Georgie was not the best subject for me this evening. And neither was Karen, come to think of it.

"You know she'd be a darn sight better off here, with family. I mean just look at you two."

Trying to keep the swelling emotion out of my voice, I coughed before I could reply. "It's going to be okay Mom, don't worry. We should get home," I said cutting off any debate.

Softening somewhat, she handed over the box of cookies, I thanked her and kissed my mom's cheek farewell.

Getting Kadee home I set about the task of relaying the news of her mother's arrival and her early departure. With a heavy sigh I sat her down and began.

"Kadee, honey. We've had a great time this week haven't we?"

"Uh huh," she replied with a smile, though I could see her child like intuition already knowing that daddy had bad news. "I don't want to go back. I want to stay here. Forever."

Her small little remark struck me like a sharp arrow in the heart, I didn't want her to go back either I wanted to keep her and hold her forever too.

"I know, sweetie. The thing is your mom is going to be picking you up the day after tomorrow."

Kadee's expression dropped as did my heart under the weight of another painful volley.

"No, no. I don't want to. Can't I stay here with you, Daddy?" Her tears were already forming while I fought mine back, the lump in my throat begging me not to say another word.

"You're going to be fine honey. You'll be back home with

your friends, you'll have your real bedroom again with all your toys."

"This is my home too. I like it better here. Georgie is my friend," Kadee sniffed through her tears.

"She is yes, and she really likes you. But Georgie has her life, and you have to go home. I promise I am going to be with you as soon as I can, I love you so much baby girl." I hugged her close as she began to sob. "It's okay. It's going to be okay," I said, wondering if I was lying to my little girl. How could it ever be okay when I was thousands of miles away from her?

"Can we see Georgie?" Kadee asked after what felt like a lifetime of tears.

"I don't think we can see her tonight. But I promise you'll see her tomorrow, though." Somehow...

CHAPTER 18

Georgie

What a turn my day took, I'd arrived back from my lunch all ready to make the most of my life. I was ready to get to work on the house, I was ready to sort things out with Derek, and it sounded like I would be able to point him in the right direction for custody.

But what turned out to be our roughest meeting yet out there in the rain had left me stunned. I certainly wouldn't be going over to his house as arranged tonight. I even steered clear of the front of the house avoiding looking over to his and ignoring the mess he'd left outside my front door.

Maybe it would be best if he was moving away. We weren't right for each other, too different, wanted different things. Too hot, clashing when things got heated. And he should be with Kadee if that was what he wanted, and really there was was no question about where he stood on that.

Though I still couldn't quite shake the gnawing feeling that I wanted him too despite the way we argued.

Needing some outlet for my pent up rage, I went about demolishing the drywall in the back bedroom that needed replacing. I wouldn't be replacing it completely today but whatever, I needed to be doing something. What better than doing something destructive? I worked for hours, fairly pleased with my productivity, the anger slowly draining out of me.

I stood back and even allowed myself a moment of hope as I imagined the improvement to the room and considered colors for the new wall.

With my arms tired and the evening drawing in, I retrieved what food I could snack on from the dilapidated kitchen and a tub of ice scream then retreated to my bed with my laptop for some comfort TV. Though the shows did little to distract me from the thoughts of Derek and the little girl I'd become so fond of. Somehow though, I'd managed to drift off to sleep. But that wasn't much comfort, what with Derek making appearances in my dreams.

Morning arrived with a chorus of bird noises accompanied by a clattering from downstairs. The sun was barely up and the world outside seemed peaceful and yet there was that noise again. Coming from inside my house. I listened carefully incase I'd just dreamt it, but no, sure enough there it was again the unmistakable sound of things being moved in the kitchen below.

The sudden panic and realization that someone was in the house made me sit bolt upright in bed. Adrenaline rushed around my body, growing intense, as I thought about what I would do with an intruder prowling my house. My phone was regrettably downstairs, but I had to do something. I couldn't just stay in bed, hiding.

Steeling myself I crept to the landing to listen. The house

was quiet again. I grabbed up my discarded hammer from the back bedroom and edged my way down step by step, carefully avoiding the loose creaky boards I'd come to know. Peering over the banister, my heart jolted as I saw who it was.

"Kadee! What are you doing here?" I exclaimed with shock as well as complete relief when I spotted her in the kitchen doorway.

"Morning, Georgie," she called out in her typically charming manner.

"Where's your dad, Kadee? You shouldn't be here, should you?"

"He's asleep. He promised I could see you today."

"Okay, but you shouldn't go out on your own," I said trying to decipher Kadee's explanation. His promise surely hadn't involved Kadee alone in my house at this time of the morning.

"Can we make pancakes for him? It will be nice. I think my daddy is sad," she said, clutching a bottle of syrup she must have brought with her.

I wasn't ready for the swell of emotion this triggered. Why was he sad? Was it because of me and my stupid outburst, that I was starting to regret? I couldn't believe this little girl had gone out of her way in the obvious hope of mending things. Maybe it wouldn't hurt, the idea of her waking up her father with pancakes would be great. Derek obviously had a lot on his plate and it seemed to be affecting Kadee now too. I could put aside my disappointment with him for just a moment, what mattered now was this helpless darling girl before me.

"Okay, I think I have the stuff. But we have to quick so I can take you straight home. He'll worry if he knows your gone. He's still asleep you say?"

"Uh huh," Kadee nodded confidently, "still snoring."

I was quickly wrapped up in the delight of Kadee's company as we set to work. She giggled at the mess I made as we rushed the mixture, then laughed even more as I promptly dabbed of mixture on her nose. When we were plating up the batch she quietened and threw her arms around my legs tightly. Was she crying?

"Hey Kadee, come now. What's wrong?"

"Nothing," she replied unable to look at me.

"Don't worry he won't be mad, but we better be quick. Are you ready to take these back to your dad?"

She nodded, wiping her face. As we made our way out of the back door we could already hear the yells from across the street. My heart sank. We hadn't been quick enough.

"Kadee! Kadee!" It was Derek and he sounded frayed with panic.

I gripped Kadee's hand firmly and increased our pace. "Come on."

We rounded the house into view to see Derek venturing across the street. The look of relief immediate on his face, his tense shoulders slumped and he was rushing toward us in his bare foot disarray.

"Kadee, you can't do that. I was terrified."

"We made pancakes. I wanted to surprise you."

"Well thank you honey, but never go off like that again," he implored, hugging her.

"I'm so sorry, she just turned up. Then wanted to make pancakes... I thought it would be okay. I was bringing her back, she was safe with me I hope you know," I said, rambling with sudden guilt at the obvious distress I'd caused.

"It's okay, thank you. I'm glad she's safe. Pancakes huh?"

The panic in his voice had dwindled but he now sounded distant, he never once looked up as he spoke. His manner produced a heavy sinking feeling of sadness in the pit of my stomach that I wanted to flee from.

"Yeah," I hesitated, suddenly aware of the slight absurdity of the three of us stood in the middle of the street in our pyjamas with a plate of pancakes.

All I wanted to do now was escape the awkwardness of the moment, Kadee was safe. I felt like a complete outsider imposing on them. I handed over the pancakes, there was no way to avoid this with Kadee watching.

"Aren't you joining us, Georgie? Please," Kadee asked sweetly grabbing for my hand.

I withdrew my hand more abruptly than I had planned to Kadee's dismay. The bright smile on her face faded as I tried to settle my emotions. But I had to remember they weren't mine. They weren't my family. And I couldn't get attached any more, not when they would both probably be gone soon enough.

"Not this morning Kadee. I have to get dressed, lots to do. You go enjoy them with your dad," I said with a feigned smile.

"But—"

"Come on, Kadee. You're not even wearing shoes. Let's get you inside." Derek nodded to me in what I presumed was approval, or was it farewell? Either way it was clear he didn't want me spending the morning with them. I responded to Kadee's enthusiastic wave, half-heartedly raising my hand, then turned to walk back home, my heart breaking with each step I took away from them.

CHAPTER 19

Derek

This was it, the last day. My last hours with Kadee, and I had no idea when I would see her again. Even if I could put my house flipping plan back into action it would be months before I was in any position to move after the setback I'd had with the house across the street. Georgie's house, I reminded myself. That was something else I had to do… I needed to apologize. She had every right to be mad at me, but I just doubled down on frustrations and took it out on her.

Kadee moped around the house with her bear Herbert in her arms. It was as if she didn't know where she belonged anymore, restless with anxiety. It was breaking my heart, as was how I had left things with Georgie. She had been a ray of hope that I'd fallen for, but the dream of the three of us had no place in reality. It had merely been a passing fantasy. And it was time to get back to the real world. Which now involved selling up moving west, watching my daughter grow up and being there for her, how could there be any other future? I would be forced to make do with whatever house or apartment I could get out there. Would even probably need to rent at least for a little while, throwing money down the drain. Long gone was the dream of having the same kind of setup I had here, it would cost too much. Nearly four times the price the last time I checked similar properties.

Kadee was all packed up, her presence in the house had been hidden away in the back pack, as well as a few bags that contained extra pieces, toys, clothes, she'd accumulated in the relatively brief period she'd been with me.

Letting my eyes drift over her room, I sensed how empty and silent it would feel in the coming days. I thought of her new bike sitting dormant in a corner of the garage, becoming rusty from the lack of use, the pads no longer needed. My brave girl had proven she didn't need them anymore. But there wouldn't be moments where I could look out the window and see her riding happily up and down the street. I so wanted to hear her giggle echoing through the house, see her bright smile, but there was no mood for these things today.

Karen arrived a little early than expected, just before two. She and her new husband Brian got out of their expensive hire car and looked around, noses turned up at the small-town neighborhood, picket fences and well-established trees. I watched from beside my curtain in the lounge window. They had a tanned and smug glow of people returning from a sunny paradise. Disdain in their eyes for boring normality that they had returned to. I did not get on with my ex—nevermind her new husband—at the best of times, her stubborn and fickle hostility, his pretentious disregard for anything he deemed below him. In a way, they suited each other but I did not know how my little Kadee endured it all and remained so sweet.

I considered how I could get through this with as little interaction as possible. I imagined a hostage like exchange in the driveway, all of us keeping our distance, where I had to let go of Kadee but got nothing in exchange. Karen, however, was already advancing toward the front door and I no option but to get this over and done with before my heart broke any more. I called to Kadee upstairs, then faced the music.

"Hey how about that, we're early," were Karen's first words.

Yeah how about that, I thought, you couldn't even give me an extra five minutes. Selfish bitch.

"Karen, Brian," I greeted them each joylessly.

"Hey Derek, how you doing? Place looks great, smaller than I remember though," Brian replied, apparently oblivious to the gravity of the situation for everyone else.

"So where is she?" asked Karen with characteristic abruptness. "We really need to get going again. This was only meant to be a pitstop."

"She should be coming down. Kadee, sweetie!" I turned to call up the stairs again.

Kadee appeared this time standing at the top to stare down at everyone. She dragged her backpack in one hand along the floor and Herbert dangled from her other hand, he hung there forlornly. Herbert looked like a bear that had given up on everything as well, ready to have the stuffing plucked out of him.

"Kadee, come on. We have a plane to catch. We can't be late," Karen called up to her.

Kadee started her slow descent while my gaze narrowed on Karen's cold features. I was trying to remember when I had ever heard her use any term of endearment for our daughter. She generally just barked commands and stubbornly expected results.

"Hurry now, Kadee, we don't have all day," Brian said with an impatient sigh. "Come and see the shiny car. We might upgrade to this model when we get back," he added. What an oh so helpful contribution, I thought bitterly.

My anger rose at their soulless attempts to herd my baby girl away from me.

"I can't believe you're taking her away this week. You seriously don't know how much this sucks," I found myself saying with the rising anger in my voice.

"Oh, relax Derek. We'll be out of your hair shortly, if only little madam here gets a move on," Karen responded with a dismissive wave of her hand. But the tap of her foot clearly indicated her impatience. "What is wrong with her? Have you been feeding her sugar? She's all lethargic."

Ignoring her last comment I turned to face her. Blocking Karen from moving any further into the house. "No, you can't wave this off. Are you even listening? No, of course not. Why would you listen to anything that isn't about Karen's perfect little life? Well, I've had just about enough of it. I thinks it's about time I fought for my daughter."

Kadee paused motionless halfway down the stairs as the volume of our voices quickly escalated.

"Let's try and keep this civil shall we?" said Brian. He was always looking to avoid any conflicts, not out of concern for others but more for his own sanity, I expected. "Kadee, let's go. Right now!" he added his tone serious and scolding.

"Really, you want to fight for her now? You've never fought for anything in your life. You have no idea how to raise a child."

Brian brushed past us and ventured up the stairs as we glared at each other.

"Come on, Kadee, let's go," he said as he tried to grab her hand and pull her down the stairs.

"Get your hands off my daughter, right now."

He stepped away and held up his hands. "Just trying to help. How about I go upstairs and check to see if she's left anything behind?"

"Good idea!" Karen and I both shouted at the same time as we glared at each other.

"Want to help me, Kadee?" he said to her. She merely nodded but then raced back upstairs.

Breaking the tension, I stepped outside not wanting Kadee to hear us arguing. Karen followed behind and I quickly closed the door. Karen took a step back maintaining the distance between us.

"Well, I'm going to fight now," I hissed, picking up where we'd left off. "She's my daughter too, and I'm a good father. You just don't let me have the time with her. But I have rights, Karen. And it's time to put a custody agreement on the table."

"Fine, fight all you want. Do you think it'll make any difference? You won't win," she yelled back at me, her tone defensive and angry at the mention of custody.

"We'll see wont we."

I still had no real idea what I was getting into, but the one glimmer of hope that Georgie had inspired in me burned now like a bright torch leading the way in a dark tunnel. I could remodel a house from top to bottom, but I had always felt out of my depth with lawyers and the like. All that law stuff was far beyond my understanding. But now I was ready to do whatever it took.

"Well, looks like she's not going anywhere yet," Brian said as he reappeared on the porch. "She's locked herself in the bathroom and wont come out."

∽

Shaken from our hostilities by a sense of concern, we all ventured inside to investigate. *Good girl,* I thought. I wanted to laugh at Kadee's ingenuity, but managed to keep a straight face. I led the way upstairs and we huddled around the bathroom door. Karen and I squatted close by listening for movement inside.

"Kadee. Honey, it's dad. Are you okay?" I asked softly.

"Uh huh," came the quiet response.

"Are you going to come out?" I continued.

"No!" Kadee cried out with a sob.

"Kadee, this is silly. If you don't come out right now, I will loose my temper."

"Go away!"

"Don't you want to go home?" added Karen, her voice taking on a sickly sweet tone, that did little to disguise her annoyance. If that was her best effort at appeasement we were going to be here for a long time.

"No, I hate you. Leave me alone! I want to say here with Daddy!"

Karen threw her hands up in exasperation and looked back at Brian who had arrived to stand silently behind us. He met Karen's look with a shrug as he leaned on the banister. These people really did make useless parents, filled to the fucking brim with compassion and patience.

"You've turned her against me."

"I have done no such thing! Trust you to think like that. Don't even start with that bullshit. You've pretty much done that all yourself," I replied keeping my voice low so Kadee couldn't hear our conversation. "Have you ever considered that she's unhappy in California with you?" Without waiting for an answer I turned back to the door. "Kadee sweetheart?"

I said, listening closely to the muffled sniffs I could hear. "What do you want to do honey?"

"I want to see Georgie," was her reply.

I squatted there stunned by the unexpected request, not knowing if it would be possible and if it would even be advisable.

"Who the hell is Georgie? Her bear?" Karen asked, her exasperation returning to hostility with this new curve ball she had been thrown from behind the bathroom door.

"No not a bear. She's our neighbor. It might help," I said getting up.

Karen stood up as well with a tinge of bewilderment on her face looking to Brian for support. But he merely stood there, blank faced, staring at the wall, thoroughly bored with the domestic situation he'd found himself in. I bet he didn't even want kids.

"If it's going to help, I'll go get her. If not, maybe I can just talk to Kadee alone and we can get this solved?" I said, lowering my voice again away from the door.

Karen shrugged. "Do whatever the hell you want, break the door down if you have to. We're going to miss our plane because of that little brat."

My fists tightened. How could she ever think of our daughter in that way? Had she even met the kid or spent time with her? Yes sometimes she'd have normal outbursts expected of a five year old but a brat? Hell, no. I let out a long, hot breath through my nostrils and decided now was not the time to go to battle. One of us would surely end up at the bottom of the stairs if I did.

"Kadee, I'll be right back okay?" I announced back at the door then left the couple muttering to each other.

I rushed over to Georgie's and glanced disapprovingly at the state I had left her steps in. I had so much to mend I didn't really know how or where to start. I'd hoped to keep my distance, letting things smooth themselves out over time, and then maybe once I had things sorted with Kadee I could make amends. However, thanks to Kadee, I was already involving Georgie again. I headed to the back door and knocked. Georgie met me with a stern look.

"What do you want? I'm not really talking to you. You still haven't fixed the mess you made.

"Hey, I know and I'm sorry," I said hesitantly, "and this may be a little awkward… I know we have other things we should probably be talking about. But Kadee is pretty upset and I think you could help. She's asking for you."

Georgie's brow furrowed. "Me?"

"Yeah, I know," I said with a smile. "Took me by surprise too. But ever since you two met, there's been this little bond. She adores you so much."

"I feel the same."

"But I have a bit of a parental nightmare occurring right now. Karen is here, her mother, to take her home but Kadee's locked herself in the bathroom, and she asked for you. I don't want to have to put you on the spot, but if you could just say hello and talk to her, maybe she'll come out. She's leaving today you see." My voice broke a little as the last words caught in my throat. There was something about telling Georgie the bad news that made the emotions well up inside me.

Concern flashed across her face and her defensive posture loosened.

"Okay, should I come over now?"

"Please, it will only take a minute. I hope."

"Fine, I can spare a minute for Kadee."

We walked quickly back across the street, deep in our own thoughts. I was doing my best to fix things here and the conclusion that awaited me was Kadee being taken away, it hardly seemed fair.

"Is she really leaving today?" Georgie asked just before we entered the house.

"That's the plan, well, that's her mother's plan."

We entered and headed upstairs. Bypassing Karen and Brian who were busy discussing something in the lounge. "You left her alone?" I yelled and shook my head, ignoring their surprised glances. Karen then ventured to the foot of the stairs to study us, or perhaps study Georgie more closely. The woman our girl has asked for. I saw the quick narrowing of her eyes and scorn on her face, but paid it little mind. I didn't care one iota if Karen was jealous of Georgie.

Georgie and I took up our positions squatting either side of the locked bathroom door.

"Honey, Georgie's here," I announced.

"Hey honey," Georgie whispered.

"Hi," Kadee said after a pause and a muffled sniff.

"What's wrong? How about you come on out so we can talk?" Georgie implored softly.

"But I don't want to go."

"I know, but your daddy looks scared and sad. He needs a hug. You should come out, things will be okay."

"Yeah, honey I'm going to work things out for you. For us both. I promise. I'm going to make sure we get to see each other more."

"You promise?"

"Cross my heart sweetie," I replied immediately, instinctively making the gesture on my chest.

"I saw it, Kadee, he crossed his heart," Georgie added, "you really have to come out now."

"Do *you* promise?" Kadee asked again for Georgie's benefit.

Georgie rolled her eyes playfully. "Yes honey, I cross my heart too. Your daddy and I will do anything to make you the happiest girl alive."

We both waited through the silence, then after a while we heard some shuffling movement from inside. I looked up at Georgie with hope, she nodded as the door latch was released. I took Kadee up into my arms immediately when she appeared and she clung on tightly.

"There she is," Georgie said, ruffling her hair. "Such a brave girl."

"Is this nonsense over now?" demanded Karen as she headed up the stairs.

Kadee clung onto me tighter the closer her mother approached.

"Yes, this is over. But she isn't going anywhere today."

Karen looked from me to Georgie with contempt.

"I better go," Georgie quickly said. "Kadee, you're going to be fine. I'll see you later, okay?"

She edged her way past Karen on the stairs. For a fleeting second, I almost secretly wished that there was time for a match up between the two of them, a battle of wills and wit. I had to wonder how Karen would fair if Georgie's fierce sarcasm and temperament was let lose upon Karen. But it was probably best for everyone involved if Georgie kept a lid on that side of her personality. Karen was already on the brink of meltdown, from the telltale fire in her eyes. I skirted past Karen as she fumed silently and carried Kadee downstairs.

Karen followed, stomping, preparing for battle, ready to persist with her demands.

"Kadee are you coming or not?"

"Not!" my daughter blurted.

"Fine. Be a naughty girl. Stay with your father let's see how long he puts up with your antics. How about we leave you here and you can fly back on your own again? Is that what you really want?"

Kadee lifted her head from my shoulder to nod furiously. Her mother growled in desperation.

"Babe, we need to get going. We can work something else out later." Brian said, moving to her while pointing dramatically at his watch.

"You know what, this has been a big waste of our time. We'll go, but it's your responsibility to get her home now, Derek. You hear me? And if you don't you'll be hearing from our lawyers."

"Not a problem," I said, still rocking Kadee in my arms.

After some lack luster farewells. Kadee refusing to say goodbye to her mom, even when I insisted, Karen and Brian stormed off back down the drive and with an excessive slamming of car doors they left.

"Thank you, Daddy."

CHAPTER 20

Georgie

For a good two days I worked hard on the house. Good was a relative term, however. It helped keep me occupied of course, making some decent progress, clearing out old fixtures and replacing them with new, but I couldn't help but find that I was only concentrating this hard on one aspect of my life, so I didn't have to deal with anything else. Purposely burying my head in the sand.

And perhaps it wasn't just me that was avoiding dealing with the heavy stuff, as I'd not even bumped into Derek or Kadee.

My brief insider's look into the family drama the other day had been interesting and somewhat uncomfortable. I'd barely been there for a couple of minutes but I could already tell by the way his ex, Karen, sneered at me and was almost dismissive toward Kadee that she was a real piece of work. I left feeling shaken... sorry for Kadee who was such a kind hearted, bright young girl, that she had to deal with a mom who almost looked right through her. Who didn't have time for her. And who treated her like a burden. God, I knew all too well what that was like.

I shouldn't be judge and jury when it came to child welfare —hell, I wasn't a mother, I didn't know the difficulties that came packaged with it—but anyone who spent so much as a few moments in the fractured family's presence would know that Kadee would be so much better off with her father, who doted on her like she was the most precious gift he could ever receive. He would, if he could, wrap the whole world in cotton wool, get out his handyman's file and smooth down life's cruel, sharp edges. All to keep his baby girl safe and sound.

But it sounded like he wouldn't get much of a chance to be a father, if Karen got her way.

This only made my heart ache when I thought about his situation. What was he going to be like once Kadee left? I couldn't bear to think about it. There was so little I could do, besides I told myself I wasn't going to get involved any more. It wasn't my place… He would obviously come to me if he needed me and he hadn't. I didn't need the distraction any longer, the house needed be my priority. I needed to do what I came to this town to do; make a home for myself that I'd never had before.

Part of me was sad he had not visited since, I missed him each day and each night as I lay alone in my bed. What was I doing even thinking about getting involved with this guy and his daughter? I had no real experience with kids. Kadee was sweet but long term what would it mean? I blamed Fiona naturally, she had always got me into some kind of trouble over the years and yet her advice still always sparked me into action.

So for the two days I got real busy with the house. I

studied the book Derek had gifted me what seemed like weeks ago, and which turned out to be a great help. I'd stripped down and painted the dining room, and somehow, amid a string of curses and expletives managed to install new baseboards, and wall lights.

As the tidiest room in the house it felt good to have a pristine area, devoid of complications. Someplace I could really think now that all the clutter, dust and mess had been swept away.

This morning I had started early, hanging my new picture frames and adding all the decorative touches that even Derek's immaculate abode lacked. With the finishing touches in place I stood back to admire my handy work.

"Not bad girl, not bad," I congratulated myself, letting the moment of accomplishment wash over me. It made me realise I could do this. I could actually have a life in this place, could do anything I put my mind to as long as I took it one step at a time. If only the same could be said about my love life.

But no rest for the wicked. Must keep the momentum flowing forward. I wanted to keep busy and planned my next tasks as I nursed a cup of coffee. I'd given up on tackling the half-finished porch steps until the weather turned for the better. So staying inside was my plan, and visited each remaining room to figure out what else I needed to order in. If I was to continue today I would need more supplies. I had become a regular at the local hardware store and the owner Edgar was at least a friendly face.

Derek's place looked quieter than usual as I sprinted for my truck, my head low, hunched trying to keep from the drizzle. There was no sign of his familiar truck on his drive, he was obviously out somewhere with Kadee. Though since the drama I had not been paying much attention and had lost track of their comings and goings. It did my state of my mind no good to watch and wonder.

A clean, simple break would be better for all concerned.

Yet when I reached my truck, I found Kadee's bear, Herbert, sitting on my windscreen, a little soggy. Maybe it was some silly signal from Kadee that she missed me? I shook the bear trying to free it of the excessive water on its fur then placed him on the passenger seat, directing the blowers on him to help get him dry.

"I bet you're missing her, huh?" I said quietly to Herbert. "Me too. Me too."

No matter her intentions, innocent or otherwise, I would have to return it and decided I would take him back later, once he was good as new again.

EDGAR GREETED me over his newspaper from his usual position, sat behind the counter of the hardware store.

"Morning dear. You just can't get enough of this place can you? Maybe I should set up some kind of loyalty card?"

"Do you blame me? It is the best hardware store in town, isn't it?"

"True enough... being that it's the only one," Edgar chuckled to himself and turned the page of his paper.

I claimed a basket and dove into the aisles for the things I needed. When I arrived back at the counter, Edgar folded his paper, obliging me with his full attention.

"You fixing up the old Cottle's place ain't ya, over on Chestnut Grove?"

"Yeah that's right, you know it?" I asked as I started to empty my supplies onto the counter.

"Not really just heard about the sale in passing. I know

Derek across the way well enough you see. Good fellow, must be one of my best customers."

"We've crossed paths," I replied not wanting to delve into the complications of our relationship. "His place is an inspiration."

"Yep, he's done wonders on that place. You should've seen it before he got his hands on it… a shame really."

"How do you mean?"

"Well, he's gone now. Last I heard he's headed west with his daughter."

"What? No, that can't be right."

"Yep, my wife's the realtor. She's already been sorting out the paperwork to sell the house and I saw him this morning all packed up in the truck heading out of town."

"Seriously, when was this?" I demanded, an irrational panic had risen from the pit of my stomach.

"Not much more than an hour ago. All seems sudden to me."

"Very," I agreed, stepping away from the counter. The panic had turned to nausea, I just turned and ran from the store leaving all my purchases behind.

"Hey, do you want me to—"

I didn't hear the end of Edgar's question as I fled outside taking a deep breath. Jumping in the truck my first thought was getting home. Maybe there had been a note, something I'd missed? Herbert watched me with concern from the passenger seat.

"Oh, Herbert… God, you're a farewell present aren't you?"

Herbert merely stared back at me with his glossy amber eyes.

When I was met by the stillness back at Derek's house I picked up and hugged Herbert. This was really it, all the dreams of the past week felt crushed like distant memories. I didn't even know what I was doing... I got out of the car and found myself hammering on Derek's door. I just had to check, to make sure. Trying to find an sliver of hope. Maybe Edgar was mistaken...

I was rapidly filling up with regrets and disappointments. Why had I not gone over to see how the were, not spent time with them during their last days? Why had I left things as I had? But why had they not said goodbye either?

To hell with clean breaks, I wanted nothing more than to see then again now. Would give anything for Derek's truck to come trundling around the corner. But as I looked down the street, waiting for a miracle, nothing happened. They were gone, and they'd taken my heart with them.

CHAPTER 21

Georgie

After dragging myself away from Derek's house, I slumped into the tatty old armchair in my lounge and that was where I'd remained. I was not sure how many hours had passed and I couldn't find the will to care.

All the miserable thoughts circled through my head, on repeat, unable to put a halt to the spiral I was heading down. I mulled over what could have been and what I would of done different. He was gone from my life forever, and I didn't even have his number. What I wouldn't give to have his arms around me again right now.

A knock on my door startled me.

I sat up rubbing my sore, red eyes. My initial thought was, Derek was back. I imagined jumping into his embrace as I pulled open the door, kissing him so much that he couldn't get a word in edgewise. We'd laugh, we'd talk. We'd kiss some more and we'd make up. Everything would go back to normal, and he would help mend my heart.

But it was never that simple. It made no sense that he would be at my door, did it?

Tentatively, I got up and slowly turned the door handle.

"Hey… Oh dear, you look rough. What the hell happened to your face?"

"Fiona," I gasped, letting all my hopes escape with the breath I'd held.

"Well yeah, who else were you expecting? You forgot about our lunch date, didn't you? And aside from your face, what the hell happened to your steps? I nearly rolled my ankle trying to climb up."

"It's not Mount Everest, Fiona," I grumbled, as I tried to imagine her clambering onto the porch as she must have done. But that was the least of my concerns.

"Someone has an attitude… not even a hello?"

"God, sorry. It's been a crazy couple of days."

"You're not forgiven yet. Come on then, tell me all about it," Fiona said ushering me inside.

She made tea while I rambled until my mouth went dry, about the occurrences of the past two days. Derek's ex, the house up for sale, their sudden disappearance. My stupid argument with him, getting angry over him only trying to help fix up my porch. Why had I been so bloody relentless? I should've swallowed my pride and asked him to help me… but no, not me, I couldn't do that. So fucking stupid.

"It's all gone to shit. And I think it's all my fault."

"Oh no it's not. He just doesn't know your reasons."

"Exactly. It's my fault. I didn't tell him!"

"That's easily fixed. You're not losing him that easy," Fiona said confidently with a quirk of an eyebrow.

Here we go again, I thought with a strange mixture of dread and hope; more of Fiona's motivational advice.

"You want to chase him down don't you? That'll be so epic, like the movies!"

"I'm sure it would, but I have no idea where he went. California is a big place, you know."

"Don't be a smart ass. Let me think. There has to be a way…" she said, trailing off as her mind set to work.

I considered her words for a while, it sounded ridiculous but Fiona always made things sound feasible and completely within reach. As if I only had to do one simple thing to make my dreams come true. To reach out and touch the stars. But this was reality, and my feet were firmly planted on the ground.

"Do you not have any clue? Surely he mentioned something… Maybe where his ex was living?"

"I don't know, if I did I can't remember," was the best response I had at the moment. "I don't even know where to start."

"Where there's a will, there's a way, babe. You rack that little brain of yours, I might have an idea."

"Wait. Kadee did mention where her new stepdad worked. He's some kind of big shot dentist I think. Dentist to the stars… She called it Reed medical or something."

"Close enough, time to get your Google on, girl! And I've probably got the air miles you'll need once we know exactly where you need to go."

WAS I REALLY DOING THIS? Was I about to chase a man across the country and declare… declare what? My love? Tell him I needed him and that he should come back… abandon his daughter and be with me instead? I groaned just thinking how selfish the idea was. But I had to at least tell him how I felt, right? Maybe somehow we'd find a solution, for Kadee to return too.

I had no idea what I could expect, I just wasn't going to wake up another day not knowing. I grabbed my hastily packed case and rushed out the door to hurry for my flight. I flung my case in the back seat and was about to jump in the front when I heard someone driving up behind me. I presumed it was the mailman because of the time of day but when I turned I saw the back of Derek's truck pulling into his drive. My heart lurched and I braced myself, pressing a hand against the steel of my car. Unable to believe my eyes.

Stunned, I could only blink in his direction. *What on earth?*

Derek got out and started toward me. His look weary, tired eyes, his hair ruffled as if he'd been up all night. But his smile grew as he approached. All the emotions of the past days suddenly collided together within me. Then a rush of violent, vulnerable anger burst free.

"Where the hell have you been? I thought—" I yelled, choking back the tears. "What's going on?"

My sudden outburst stopped him in his tracks as a look of puzzlement crested onto his face.

"Have you any idea what I was about to do?" I continued, practically shaking with relief that he was here.

"Erm, no?" he replied with a half shrug and an indulgent smile. That only made me more irate. How could he smile at me like that when I'd been such a mess? Desperate and anxious, going out of my mind… all because I was falling in love.

"Of course not… did you even think for a minute that—"

"Think about what?" he asked with clear confusion.

"About me!" I yelled. My hands flew to my face to cover my eyes and the hot tears that tumbled free.

"I haven't stopped thinking about you," he replied, yelling to match my loudness, his irritation clearly rising.

"You have a funny way of showing that, disappearing like that leaving me to think—"

My sentence was cut off as he closed the space between us and took hold of me in his strong arms, kissing me deeper than he ever had before. His passion immediately silenced all my doubts and fears, all my pain.

I was swept up in the intense whirlwind as he lifted me almost off my feet. I met his kisses with my own sudden immense desire. Our lips, our bodies, had missed each other and they were making up for the last couple of days apart.

"I thought you had left town. For good," I whispered breathlessly with a brief pause, "I thought I'd lost you."

"Not a chance. I flew Kadee home. I got the red eye back this morning. I couldn't wait to see you."

"She's gone?" I replied, my heart faltering at the news.

He nodded.

"I'll miss her."

"Me too…"

With sadness in his eyes, Derek took hold of my face with his warm hands and kissed me once again. Lips melting against mine. Then he looked deep into my eyes. The flood of emotion and relief I felt combined with the sudden intensity of his advance had sparked a now roaring fire. He could clearly see it in my eyes and the look he returned only fanned the flames.

I was about to lean in to kiss him again when he lifted me up into his arms. I flung my arm around his neck for support as he carried me around the side of the house. I studied him and stroked his face, grazing over the stubble on his chin. Then my fingers found their way into his hair.

Derek dropped me by the back door where I quickly opened up and let us in. His hands were on me the whole time, and by the time we'd moved into the kitchen he had hold of me again. I was pinned against the counter as his urgent roaming hands explored me and our lips met fiercely. He was tugging open the buttons on my top as I shoved aside the stuff on the counter, not caring as the items clattered to the floor. He lifted me onto the surface and pushed up to me as I wrapped my thighs around him. I looked into his heavenly eyes now at my level.

"I'm sorry I didn't tell you what was happening. I've was caught up with everything going on, and I wanted to be sure of things. I never wanted you to think I'd left without even saying goodbye."

"Are you sure of things now?" I asked, not certain what he meant but knowing from his smile it was something good.

"More than I have ever been," he replied running his fingers delightfully into my hair.

He tugged open my blouse, his teasing fingers wandered up and down my skin followed by delicious tingles that had me gasping for more. I ripped open his shirt in return wanting to stroke his firm chest. His warm lips sank into my neck as our hands worked over each other with appreciation.

I tugged at his belt while he kicked off his boots. He threw down his jeans and grabbed my shoes slipping them off and discarded them in the corner as well. A sense of urgency overtook us. He couldn't wait and neither could I.

Derek pushed up close to me again sliding his hands down my tummy to take hold of the waist button on my jeans, I smiled and watched his eyes with anticipation. He unbuttoned me roughly and helped me wriggle my ass out of the jeans, then landed me back onto the cold counter. Once they were dealt with he then slid his hands all the way back up my legs achingly slowly until they were back on my hips.

I let out a quiet whimper and coiled my legs around his to hold him to me, indulging in the warmth of his skin close to mine. I slid out of my blouse and threw it around his neck, taken hold of it both sides I pulled him back to my lips. We kissed slowly and deeply while he worked me out of my bra and started caress my exposed breasts lovingly. I was in rapture now holding him tight, the smell of him, the touch of his fingers consuming me. I didn't want this feeling to end. I kept stroking at his rippling muscles as his lips wandered from my neck to play across my breasts. He lavished them with more attention than I might of imagined. His lips and firm tongue teased around them, and they hardened in response.

As desire overtook me I reached down to the hard bulge in his shorts rubbing and stroking until I elicited a moan from Derek's mouth. I smile tugged at my lips, my strokes harder, more insistent now.

When he bit my taut nipple I pulled his rigid cock free and with a firm grip worked it. We went back and forth like this, both eager, breathless, and wanting to one up the other as our hands explored our bodies.

Until Derek stilled. I had him right where I wanted him.

He stood up taller, closing his eyes in pleasure. I continued to watch his face as I took hold of him with both hands, gripping him lightly, my thumb dancing across his swollen head. He was rock hard beneath my fingers now.

I tugged and worked him with horny mischief thinking of him inside me. I felt so wet with anticipation that I couldn't bear it. Almost as if we'd shared the same thought, he drew back and took a grip of my knickers. I helped him again with the wriggle of my ass and away they went together with his shorts. Leaning me back, teased himself up to my wet waiting pussy.

His bulbous thick head rested on my clit, pulsing in tandem with the furious beat of my own musical cacophony. With a look of determination, Derek controlled the end of his cock like he was wielding a pen. Drawing himself across me as if he were writing a love letter to my pussy. Tentatively he skimmed the bundle of nerves, watching me squirm when I jolted from the pressure, biting my lip as I moaned through the pleasure.

The anticipation of his slow disciplined actions made me ache. I rested my hand onto of his, hoping to urge him to press himself between my folds, but he held firm, a devilish look in his eye.

"Derek," I pleaded, "I can't wait." Digging my heels into his nice hard ass I tried again, hoping to encourage him to relent, to take me.

"You want this?" he said as he pressed the weighty meat of his cock against my clit again.

"Yes... oh god. You know I do."

He drew his weapon back only to replace it with an excited thumb, vibrating hard and fast. My head and shoulders rolled back, eyes wide as I looked up at the ceiling but unable to focus. Everything was blurry as his fingers worked their magic on me. I could feel my heart beat pounding around my temples, my finger tips, even my toes. I gripped the edge of the counter trying to hold on... until I realized I didn't have to hold on. Not anymore. He was here. He was mine.

We could do this all day.

My body juddered as a throaty scream roared out of me. But his thumb wasn't finished with me yet, he tapped and teased my bud till I panted and moaned his name. Then when I finally thought I was spent Derek cruelly reminded me we'd only just begun.

Holding onto my hips he drove into me. Every inch he gave me heightened my delight, and the wave of pleasure from our union only grew stronger, higher and more intense. I couldn't help but whimper at the heavenly feelings. I wrapped my arms around his neck as he thrust and rocked, working deeper into me as he did.

I let out a squeak as he scooped me up, removing me from the counter and slammed me against a wall. The one I'd planned to knock down… maybe we could kill two birds with one stone, I thought wickedly.

His rocking hips worked like a well oiled piston, firmly set on a course, unrelenting. My head swan as I hung on, squeezing him with my thighs tighter as his steady and intense motion brought my tightening insides to a boil once more.

He fucked me harder and faster now almost bouncing me off the wall, as sweat dripped from his brow. The thick muscles of his arms bulged from the exertion. As if we were doing a tour of the kitchen, my back left the cool of the wall and he swung me around to lay me flat on the table. The level of which seemed to be the perfect height, his cock inline with my horizontal hips.

I reached out with a flailing arm to steady myself with little success as I bumped my head the tops of a chairs that was tucked in beneath the table. He smiled and dragged me back to him, then with a firm grip of my thighs lifted me up.

"Maybe we should find somewhere a little more comfortable?"

"I don't care as long as you keep fucking me," I replied.

I clung to his neck again and was carried from the kitchen. He effortlessly took me up the stairs to my bed. It was still unmade from my haste that morning. He dropped me down and immediately fell into the bed beside me, not letting me out of his grasp for too long.

Spooning up behind me he lifted one of my legs and smoothly slipped inside me again. I moaned at the new angle of assault and friction as his insistent thrusting began.

His hand ran up and down my body from my thigh,

pausing to part them like butterfly wings so he could have access to my clit, then to my breasts.

Passion welled up from deep inside me, it clouded all thoughts my boiling pleasure ready to erupt. With another wild moan I escaped his embrace and rolled onto my back. Looking into his eyes with desire I lifted my knees and spread myself, welcoming him home. He shifted onto me and with a kiss was drove himself up into me once more.

Now with greater urgency and intent he rocked me on the bed. I moaned and urged him on, gripping his upper arms, ready to explode and wanting him to.

My grasp wandered and I moved my hands to his neck, pulling him down, closer, and deeper inside me and watched his eyes and his groaning face as his last slow deliberate thrusts plowed into me so deeply.

His eyes met mine as he unleashed himself deep inside my pussy. I tensed up, my walls milking him, and with the feeling of his throbbing explosion and the desire in his eyes I couldn't hold back any longer. The coil unwound with violent energy and an intense and satisfying climax raged through my body. My throat opened up, loudly praising how good he felt. He groaned to, working his still throbbing cock inside me slowly until we were spent and gasping for air... Only for our mouths, a second later, to search for each other once more.

CHAPTER 22

Derek

The sun shined through the window basking us in golden light. Georgie stirred beside me when I turned my head away from the glare.

"Morning you," she purred.

"Hello there," I replied, the warmth of the sun was matched now by the affection in her smile. I sure could get used to this, I thought as she snuggled up to me.

"So how about breakfast?" I asked.

"Not yet. We can just lay here a while, can't we?"

Wrapping my arms around her, my leg slinking between hers, I said, "Sounds perfect." It definitely felt perfect, life felt full of hope and possibility with her in my arms. She turned to press her body up against the length of mine, spooning lazily as I stroked her hair.

Today I didn't want to leave her side at all. Not even for one moment. I was hooked. I started to rack my brain for the best excuse to stay or activities for us. Naturally with her warm naked body pressed against me the urge to linger in bed all day was ever present.

"How's your day looking?" she asked, apparently following the same train of thought. "After breakfast, erm… how would you feel about fixing up the porch together?"

"Yeah, I definitely owe you that, and it's a great day for it."

"I'm sorry I shouted at you the other day about it."

With some gentle pressure I angled her face toward mine. "You don't need to apologize. I was out of line. I didn't ask and overstepped. Pun not intended."

"Thank you for saying that… I guess I find it hard to let anyone help me. Especially with this house. My first house."

"I didn't know it was your first."

"There's a lot we don't know about each other."

"Well, we can change that," I said and nuzzled her neck. "But first…"

Against the warm curves of her ass my cock pressed eagerly. She was ready for me, angling her hips, partly lifting her leg so I could slip inside. She moaned as I took her from behind with long, slow, lazy strokes. With our eyes half-closed, we drifted on a lake of euphoria, letting our bodies melt into one another.

The intensity of when we both came was unlike I'd ever experienced before. I tasted her heavy moans as they were expelled, and almost thought I could feel the colors of her soul as they flashed before my shuttered eyes. It was as if a sixth sense had been aroused when we'd woke from our dreamy intimacy and entangled ourselves.

Words were a little hard to come by as I lay back, her hair splayed across my chest as we recovered. But there was one thing that was abundant and it practically strangled my heart when I understood its profound meaning.

I'd discovered love.

After breakfast we got to work clearing up the mess outside. As if in tandem, side by side we worked fast and easy. Glancing over at each other with a knowing smile, and occasionally stealing a kiss or coping a feel.

It felt good to be mending what really signified the disarray that had developed between us. There was no chaos or confusion today, we worked well together. We laughed and teased each other in the hot sun as the new steps came together.

"Lemonade?" Georgie asked as she wiped away a bead of perspiration that sprouted on my forehead.

"Yes, please." The midday sun was taking its toll on us hard working renovators, my throat dry from the exertion. Georgie quickly returned with two tall glasses. I propped the brush that I was using against the rail and received the cool refreshment with a smile. Our eyes meeting as we raised our glasses to our mouths. I could barely take my eyes off her. Wanting to study every contour of her face, have it ingrained in my mind in case I ever had cause to be away from her for a second.

"Are you really selling up?" Georgie asked after a sip, surprising me.

I swallowed and wondered how to tackle the hard subject. "Thinking about it."

It was there for only a fleeting second, but I was a quick study and noticed immediately the slight frown that marred her forehead. I took her hand to try and ease whatever worries she had brewing.

"I don't think my plan is going to come together, though. But maybe it wasn't the right plan you know? Originally I'd hoped to offer Kadee a decent home out west, one like I have here. Grass, a garden, plenty of space. But all that costs a small fortune out there so I may have to just settle for what I can get on a budget."

"Really, *you* had a plan?" Georgie teased, though I knew she was putting a brave face on it. But I'd decided I was going to tell her the truth. No more skirting around the subject, avoiding it like it was an elephant in the room.

I flicked some of my precious lemonade in her direction, getting a pouty smile in return, before I replied. "Yes, I had a plan! I was about to renovate and flip a house around here. There's a strong market for these older houses done up."

"Like this one?"

"Yeah, exactly like this one," I replied with hesitation. I took a breath and met her gaze. "This is the one I was going to buy. But you beat me on the offer."

"Really?" Georgie absorbed this silently for moment. "No wonder you hated me."

"Well, that's an exaggeration. You pissed me off for sure when you turned up all cocky and inexperienced... and god then you broke my flashlight," I said nudging her.

"That was just as much your fault as it was mine."

I laughed. "Keep telling yourself that, butter fingers." Before she could protest or throw a retort my way, I silenced her with a kiss. I pushed a few strands of her hair off her cheeks and sighed. "It's just that this place would have been perfect."

She nodded. "I can see that," said Georgie leaning back to take in the view of the house. "There's definitely something about it."

"Yeah," I replied slowly, taking in the same view. "Not to mention the easy commute across the street."

Any anguish I'd felt regarding flipping this house, combined with Georgie's intervention now felt like nothing more than a bittersweet hiccup. I could imagine far greater things than selling this place now, specifically with Georgie in my life.

"I don't suppose you'd ever consider moving to California?" I glanced over to gauge her reaction, but it was written so clearly on her face that I needn't have tried. It was a silly thing to ask. I wished I could take it back.

Georgie gripped my hand then brought it to her lips. "I'm sorry. That's not something I could do."

"I—"

"Let me explain. This is my home now. For better or worse. I need roots." She paused, her mouth working as if she were trying to find the right words. "Derek, I've never had a home. Not a proper one. Not really. I was an army brat and it seemed like every second I was being dragged to a new place, four thin walls and a flimsy roof to call 'home'. But the sentiment was hollow… I never found where I belonged. Never felt like I had my feet on solid ground, you know?"

I nodded, trying to understand. Coming from a place that I'd barely left all my life—the house I'd grew up in, only a few miles down the road—it was hard to imagine the life Georgie had to endure.

"What made you choose Hollow Point?"

"Fiona, my friend—the one I told you about. She lives in the city. We met the year we were deciding on colleges. Then we ended up at the same one. I suppose those years were really the first step to breaking the lifelong cycle of feeling like I was just another footlocker to shipped where the army wanted. Though I still drifted for a while after I dropped out, not knowing what to do or where to go. Then my aunt Dakota died and gave me everything… a lifeline if I'm being honest."

Georgie sniffed and I gave her an encouraging squeeze.

"Then you bought this house?"

"Not right away. In the will she told me to use it to follow my dreams… to find my place. And for a second there I didn't know what that meant. To suddenly have the whole world open to me and yet not wanting to take another step. It was weird. Fiona was the one that gave me the idea," Georgie said, laughing. "Don't know what I would do without her. Probably would've drifted forever, with no purpose. Would never have met you…"

Georgie rested her head on my shoulder and sighed.

"I hope you can understand why I can't follow you to California, even though my heart longs to be with you and Kadee. I'm settled here. I feel it in my bones. I need this. The stability. This formidable house, with its strong walls, its solid base. Even if it'll take me years to get it the way I envisage it. I have to stay."

"I understand," I breathed. Wondering where we went from here. But I already knew… deep down. I wasn't going to abandon the love I'd found the moment it moved in across the street from me.

Georgie took our finished glasses and placed them on the porch, then turned with a promising smile on her plump lips.

"But, you know…" she started again, "there could be a even better way."

She bit her lip and came back to stand in front of me.

"I'm all ears."

"I think, well I think I lo—"

"I love you," I blurted. I'd been wanting to tell all morning, all afternoon. And I couldn't let another minute fly by without letting her know.

"Hey you stole my line!"

I grinned at her. "I'm sorry. I couldn't let you finish without you knowing that I loved you. That no matter what you were about to say, that I get it. Your place is here. In this battered old house that has so much promise. And that we'd figure something out, because, Georgie-baby, you moving in, stealing this house from under me, turning my world upside down, was the best thing that has ever happened to me in a very long time."

"That's good to know then, but I didn't steal… I won fair and square," she said with a playful smirk. She paused and narrowed her eyes. "Oh, good you're not going to interrupt me ag—"

"I can't make no promises there."

She batted me with her hand and I kissed her on the nose.

"Will you let me say it now?"

I nodded.

"I love you, too, you big fool," she managed to say, partly giggling. "And what if you could win Kadee back—Fiona knows all the right people… then you could stay here? With me. On this street… maybe even move in? My house is bigger than yours after all."

"Like that is it? Comparing sizes… things just got personal," I replied with a grin. "So… a new plan?"

"One we make together?"

"That does sound promising," I said, taking her into my arms, "do you think it's possible?"

"Anything's possible with you."

EPILOGUE

Georgie

*I*t was amazing what difference just two months could make in your life.

It was the height of the summer and here we were basking in our love and our new shared decision to be together.

At the last minute I stuck my tongue out at Derek, as he passed by me again, instead of pretending to trip him here in the middle of the street. He may not see the prank over the boxes and fall anyway. Perhaps moving day was enough of a strain without causing any more havoc, like a trip to the hospital for a broken wrist. But that didn't stop us from our typical playful antics, or the kisses we stole from each other when we inevitably collided as we rushed in and out of doorways. We were moving so fast, it was as if we couldn't wait for the day to be finally over and last box put in its rightful place.

But it wasn't like we were moving far.

Derek's place had sold for a great price. I did of course assign my own decorative touches and designer's eye to help boost the asking price, and within a week he received an offer and I'd been hired to dress houses by the realtor, Barbara, Edgar's wife.

We were turning out to be an amazing team, an unstoppable combination of practical and artistic skill. All three of us in fact.

"Here, Georgie!" Kadee shouted, meeting me in the doorway with a smile bigger than the box she carried.

"That looks heavy. Why don't you bring that one over, I'll grab this one?"

She blew out a breath, then gave me a serious and determined nod.

Custody of Kadee had been amazingly fast with the aid of Fiona's great lawyer friend. But mostly because the honeymoon period for Karen and Brain had been shattered by his exposed adultery and Karen's new purpose in life: Hollywood. Karen offered little resistance especially when Kadee wouldn't stop asking to go "home" for the weekend to visit her dad. Karen also was apparently now only interested in her acting career even though there did not appear to be one forthcoming.

Thankfully, Kadee seemed no worse the wear for all this turmoil going on in her life. And I felt a pang of guilt that the poor child was being shipped too and fro, across the country, until the verdict finally came down. But now that she was here, with us, she was loving her new school, making new friends, and most importantly was reunited with Herbert.

The past two weeks since her arrival the three of us had become so close knit, I could barely remember a time before we were all together. We'd become that heavenly family I had dreamed about the first night Derek had taken us out to the local restaurant.

"Wait, come here you," I said, before Kadee had the chance to skip away and get back to work. She'd insisted on bringing her toys over to my—our house by herself. I bent down and wrapped my arms around her. She indulged me then placed a kiss on my cheek. I straightened her ponytail and reattached on of the fastening of her cute little dungarees that had come loose.

"We still have lots of boxes to go."

"I know we do, but we'll get it done. Don't you worry. Did you pick out your room yet?"

Kadee nodded. "The one at the back so I can look at the garden."

I smiled, somehow knowing she would pick that one. It had the cutest window seat, perfect for a little girl to sit on and look out at the world. To read and dream. A place of her own.

"Good choice. You won't mind being next to the nursery then?" I said.

Kadee's smooth forehead wrinkled as the words filtered through her quick brain. Then her eyes went wide and she glanced down at my stomach.

Leaning in closer, she cupped her hand like we were sharing a secret—which I supposed we were—and whispered in my ear. "Georgie, do you have a baby in your belly?"

I did likewise and cupped my hand over her ear. "Yes." Then leaned backed and grinned. "Is that okay? Would you like a baby brother or sister?"

Kadee's head bobbed so fast, then she bought her hands to her mouth and giggled. "A little brother, please."

"It doesn't exactly work like that, but I'll try my best."

I saw she had more to say and waited for her to find the courage. This had been a regular theme since Kadee moved to Hollow Point for good. She was still finding her feet, a little unsure of whether she'd be told off for speaking her mind, feeling like a nuisance for merely asking questions a bright child would. But we were not Karen and Brian, we wanted to nurture our precious girl, not let her wither like a plant without light.

"Georgie, when the baby arrives will I be able to call you mommy too?"

I struggled to keep the emotion from spilling down my face, my heart almost burst from the innocence of her question.

"Baby-girl, if you want… you don't have to wait."

"Okay, Mommy," she said and threw her arms around my neck. I snuggled into her telling myself not to cry during this perfect moment. To remember it and cherish it forever.

Across the front garden, I spotted Derek coming up the path and our eyes met. He shot me a wink, causing my eyes to light up and a mischievous thought to run through my head. I whispered in Kadee's ear.

Now full of purpose Kadee sprinted towards her father.

"Daddy, daddy! Guess what?"

Derek shifted the box he was carrying to one side, and picked up Kadee with the other. "What? What have you two been whispering about?"

Kadee, unable to keep the secret any longer curled her hand in the familiar position around Derek's ear. I got to my feet, and stood waiting on the porch, studying his face.

Just like Kadee's had, his eyes sprang to life, the knowledge of what was to come dawning on him. Then the box was promptly discarded and he, with Kadee, in his arms now, approached with a cautious smile.

"Is it true, Georgie?" he whispered, his mouth dropping open.

"Of course it's true, Daddy. Mommy never lies."

Shocked Derek glanced from Kadee to me, a double whammy of information striking him. He'd wondered when Kadee might accept me as her new stepmom, but I'd told him it was far too soon. And yet Kadee was full of surprises.

"Georgie?" Derek repeated and I couldn't hold out any longer.

I moved to stand with them, hugging them both. "I'm pregnant. It's a good thing we have a spare bedroom, huh?"

"Well there goes my office," he replied, still in shock I imagined, his eyes twinkling.

"You're a handy-man aren't you? I'm sure you can build an extension... Are you pleased?"

"That's an understatement. This is the best day ever. I can't believe it. I'm going to be a dad again. I love my girls so much."

I nodded and pressed a kiss to his lips.

The weeks before Kadee's arrival had been rather memorable, as we explored each room of the house, intimately. It was hard to know if Derek and I had spent more time working on the house or cementing our relationship together. So that it was unbreakable.

We all stood for a moment longer, Kadee still in Derek's arms, my fingers entwined with his. We glanced up at the dream house that was filling up so fast, with love, with new beginnings.

It still needed a few finishing touches, but we were on the right path to make it perfect. Looking back now on that first day when I arrived on Chestnut Grove and met the loves of my life, I could have never imagined how everything could change so dramatically. How, with them, I'd finally found my place and sense of purpose.

It was so good to be home.

Thank you for reading Handy. Available Now - Bad Behavior!

Cynic. F*ck up. Outsider.
That's Jameson in a nutshell - not to mention *drool-worthy, dreamy,* and *perfect fantasy object.*

He's also my older brother's best friend and business partner.

I've had a thing for Jameson ever since I was old enough to have dirty dreams. My brother has made it crystal clear that if he catches rough, wrong-side-of-the-tracks Jameson even looking at me, someone will get hurt.

That doesn't deter me, though. I want Jameson to be my first.

And that's why my brother can never find out what happened.

Because Jameson kissed me.

No -- not kissed -- he shoved me up against a wall, possessed me, and took my breath away. Then he promptly passed out in my bed, wasted.

Now I know that Jameson wants me. I may be off limits because of my brother, but that kiss is branded in my mind.

I need another taste of Jameson.

I *crave* his brutal touch. Pinned against the wall, gasping at the feel of his body pressed against mine, crying out in pleasure and pain while he gives me everything I've dreamed about.

As long as my brother doesn't catch on, Jameson might just give me exactly what I want... and a whole hell of a lot more.

Read Bad Behavior NOW!

WANT MORE? READ AN EXCERPT FROM HOW TO LOVE A COWBOY

Pete

I closed the ledger and leaned back into the rich cherry colored leather of the desk chair. I closed my eyes and rubbed my temples, thinking about how much easier things had been when my father was around running things at Killarny Estate. It wasn't anything I hadn't become accustomed to over the years. Being the oldest of the five Killarny brothers, it was expected from birth that I would be the one to take over the day to day running of the ranch. While all the brothers were equal partners in running the ranch, it was I who was the most responsible. Ask anyone. It was also me that my dad had turned to back when my mother, Emily Killarny, had first been diagnosed with breast cancer.

At my mother's request, I took on the additional tasks that my father had usually taken care of. Most of it was business, the sort of thing that didn't capture my attention quite like the quiet, meditative work with the horses, but I knew what had to be done. Most of all, I hadn't wanted to let my mother down.

Emily Killarny was a force unto herself, but she had a kind and good heart, and above all, she loved her children. I was aware that I had a special place in her heart when she had gone out of her way to be the best kind of grandmother she could be to Emma. I'd been dejected and alone, raising a two year old daughter alone after my ex-wife, Kelly, decided one day that motherhood and married life wasn't for her. My parents had been so kind to us in the days following that abandonment, and I would forever be grateful to both of them. My mother had especially done all that she could to make sure that Emma felt safe and loved after her mother's abrupt departure.

Back then my major responsibilities had been tending to the horses, something I still loved and wished I was able to do more of, but being the oldest, and since my father had relocated to Costa Rica, I knew I had to be the one to step up to the plate. My mother's death three years prior had taken a toll on the family patriarch, and after suffering a severe bout of depression, he finally decided to make some major changes. One of those changes included leaving the states and relocating to a warmer climate, leaving the green Kentucky hills behind him in favor of sun and sand. Some days I couldn't help but feel a little jealous of that, but I knew that my heart would always be right here, wherever Emma was.

I opened my eyes again and looked at my computer screen for a moment before getting up and heading for the door, grabbing my jacket on the way. There was still a chill in the air that early in the Kentucky spring and it was invigorating to step out into the morning air, breathing in the fresh smell of new grass and the less pleasing scent wafting from the nearest barn. The smell of manure might not have appealed to everyone, but for me, it was a reminder of home and childhood.

I breathed in the air and made my way over to the stables where my brother Alex was brushing out the coat of a two year old mare.

"She looks beautiful," I said as I came up to stand on the other side of the stall door.

Alex nodded. "Siobhan is quite a looker." He brushed her russet coat to a glistening sheen that caught the early morning sun and made the horse look like a copper penny.

"You think we'll run her next year?" I asked him as I looked over the horse from nose to tail. She was beautiful, but I wasn't sure if she was one of the horses that we would end up taking to the many derbies we were involved in.

Alex shrugged. "Not sure. She hasn't been run that much, and I really think that if we had planned on doing that with her, she should have seen a little more practice at this point in her life. I think she is a great horse, but I'm not sure the derby life is the one for her. However, I do think she is going to give us a lot of talented foals."

Alex was probably the quietest of all the brothers, so hearing him talk this much was a little unusual. The only time Alex had much to say was when he was talking about a horse. Not much for words and usually keeping to himself, he was definitely the most horse whisperer like among us and was more involved with the training of individuals here at the ranch. He was so in tune with the horses that it helped to have his expertise around to help people become accustomed to green horses. While most of our horses were bred here on the ranch, we did keep a group of wild ponies from the Dakotas on one of the spreads of land that was fenced off from the rest. Alex's house was out there and visiting that part of the ranch felt like entering a wilderness. I could see why my parents had given him that parcel when they were divvying up the land to us. It fit my younger brother's personality perfectly, and he was never happier than he was when he was among the wild horses.

"Her mother is Spring, right?" I asked.

"Yeah, and her father was David's Lariat."

David's Lariat had been one of Alex's favorites. A horse that my father had acquired from a Colorado ranch when we were still very young, the horse had been a monster of an animal when we got him. He stood taller than any of our other horses but managed to be faster than almost any horse half his weight. He was a marvel and had produced many of our fastest horses. David's Lariat had died just a year before, but we still had a few of his offspring around the ranch and would likely see his influence in our derby horses for decades to come.

"Well, even if she isn't going to run for us, she's a beautiful girl, and I'm sure she'll give us a few great runners."

"What are you up to?" Alex asked as he put away the brush and stepped out of the stall to join me where I stood.

I shrugged. "Just needed to get out of the office for a little while."

"Already?" He looked at his watch. "It's early in the day. Why don't you hire someone to take care of some of the stuff you don't enjoy? That's what bookkeepers are for, after all. It would give you a break and let you have a chance to get back out here with the horses where you want to be."

Alex was perceptive with more than just the horses.

"Yeah, well, I might do that after the next couple of derbies have passed. I've got too much on my plate right now to hand it over to someone totally new."

My brother sighed and shrugged. "Whatever you say. Just don't be afraid to ask for a little help when you need it."

I gave him a firm pat on the back and continued on down through the stables, past the stalls that housed our many horses. A few of our ranch hands were leading some of the horses out to graze in the pasture, while some of them were headed to the arena and our track for training. As I exited the other end of the massive stable, I saw Emma atop her horse, Saoirse.

"How'dya do, Miss Emma Lou?"

Emma frowned at me, and I could see her brow furrowing under her helmet. I knew she hated it when I referred to her middle name, Louise, but told myself that someday she would come to think of it as endearing, so I kept up the practice.

She tossed her head back. "Saoirse and I just went out for our morning run. I was about to take her back to the stable and then head in for my lessons. Is Hetty here yet?"

I shook my head. "She wasn't there when I left the house, but there's a good chance she's arrived by now. Better hurry on back, you don't want to be late."

My twelve year old daughter beamed at me from where she sat on her horse and headed into the stable before dismounting. I watched her lead her young horse into the stall and couldn't help but notice how much she was starting to look like her mother. It wasn't a bad thing, but I did wonder how Emma would feel as she looked in the mirror and started to notice the resemblance she shared with the woman who left her—and me—behind when Emma was just a toddler.

I walked toward the pasture as I recalled the time directly after Kelly left. It had been a shock to me when it happened, but when I had a little time to think it over, nothing about it was too surprising. We had married straight out of high school, and my parents had been opposed to the match from the start. Kelly's parents were business owners in the nearest town, and ours had been the kind of wedding that made the local papers. Our courtship had been brief — we dated at the end of high school, and because I was an idiot, I had proposed to Kelly not long after graduation. We married and moved into a house here at Killarny Estate and had had a hell of a time for the first couple of years.

Kelly was wild and looking back I could tell she had been just a little too wild for me. It wasn't something I had noticed at the time, and while it was just the two of us, it was easy to forget that we were stepping into a new world that included all sorts of new responsibilities. Back then we would spend our weekends hopping around the bars in town before heading back to the privacy of our house at the ranch and going at it like rabbits. It was no surprise when Kelly got pregnant, and I was overjoyed, but she didn't seem too enthused about it. Slowly she warmed to the idea, and once Emma was born, I could see that she really did love our daughter.

Things were never the same though. Kelly never looked at me the same way, and I tried to encourage her to go see a doctor to see if what she was struggling with was postpartum depression, but she wouldn't listen.

I came home one evening to find all of Kelly's things gone, a note on the kitchen table, and Emma wailing in her playpen. I had picked up my daughter and the note and read the words through tears as Emma sniffled and buried her head against my shoulder. Kelly was gone. She apologized in the letter, said she was heading to California to pursue her dream of being an actress, and that she was going with her friend, Bud.

Bud was the guy she had dated before me in high school, and suddenly it all started to make sense. We never really heard from her after that, aside from a Christmas card or a birthday present for Emma on the years that Kelly remembered, which were few and far between.

As far as I knew, Emma had no real memory of her mother. It made me sad, but I wondered if it was for the best that she didn't know what she was missing out on. If Kelly had hung around much longer, it would have been more difficult than it already was to get Emma used to not having her mother around.

I had been so grateful to my parents for the support they were during that time, especially my mother. She had done all she could to be the maternal figure in my daughter's life, but she never stopped pressing me to go on dates and get out there again, constantly reminding me that I was still young and there was happiness out there for me if I would just go looking for it.

Her last attempt had been just a few years before she passed away when I had first hired Hetty Blackburn, a local teacher, to be Emma's tutor. The ranch was well out of the way, and it was quite a hike to the nearest school, so I had decided to homeschool Emma. It gave her a chance to be around the horses more and to study at her own pace, which was quite a bit faster than the average elementary school student, according to Hetty.

Hetty was pretty and a very sweet woman. Her black hair and blue eyes were a sort of bewitching combination that was hard to ignore, but I couldn't get back into dating; not then and not now, even though it was 10 years since Kelly walked out. Even if I hadn't already been very hesitant to date, Hetty already had one major strike against her—she knew my daughter.

I leaned against the bright white fence and watched as a group of our horses played together in the dewy field that was filled with clover. The place was even more picturesque than usual in this light. Killarny Estate was really something to be proud of, and I was so glad to have the privilege of being a part of a four generation horse ranch, the largest one in Kentucky, and now, for all intents and purposes, running the place.

WANT MORE? READ AN EXCERPT FROM HOW TO LOVE A …

One rule I had established for myself was that until I knew I could trust a woman, she would never meet my daughter. And since I wasn't in the mood to start dating yet, nothing had ever made it that far. Sure, I had been with women since Kelly—too many to count—but I was there to get what I wanted and get out. I never went out with anyone that I thought was there for more than what I was because I had more heart than that. But I didn't trust anyone to give me any more than what I was looking for at the moment. It was sex, pure and simple—though rarely pure or simple. I was there for a release, to have sex, hear them scream my name, and then leave quietly. The closest I had ever come to bringing a woman home was the Lawrence girl who I made it all the way back to the ranch with, but we never left my truck. We had made it as far as the pecan grove when I pulled over and had her right there in the cab of my pickup. When we were done, I turned around and drove her right back to her house. But that had been the last one, and that had been a long time ago now.

There was no need to complicate my life any more than it already was and I was certainly not going to bring any of these women into the life of my daughter. She had already experienced enough pain from my poor choices, and I wasn't going to do that to her again.

My middle brother, Jake, came riding up on his stallion and brought the horse to a quick halt a few feet away from me.

"Showing off?" I asked as I cocked my eyebrow at him.

He swung down off the saddle and gave the horse a pat. "This bastard is ready to run!"

Clement certainly looked like he was ready for it. His eyes were wild, but it was clear that he was happy after his morning run with Jake.

"Think about how fast he's going to be with one of the jockeys on him!"

I nodded. "We're taking him to the Waters derby, right?"

"Yup, just a couple of weeks away now."

I noted to myself that I needed to check that out on the calendar. There was still a lot left to do in preparation, and we weren't sure how many horses we would be taking. Clement was certainly on the top of the list, but I knew we needed to have a few backups. Killarny Estate had always been top of the pack as far as producing some of the fastest race horses in the country, but ever since my father had packed it up and gone to Costa Rica, it felt like we had lost some of our edge. I had no idea what it was Dad had that we didn't quite have down yet, other than the forty years of experience. What I did know was that it was crucial for us to win this derby. Things were tight, and if we were going to turn them around and maintain things the way they were around here, or if we were ever going to have any hope of making Killarny the very best again, we had to win the Waters derby.

"You coming?" Jake asked me as he brushed his reddish-brown hair back out of his face and wiped his brow with the back of his sleeve.

I looked at him bewildered. "Of course I am."

He shrugged. "Don't act like it's a given. You haven't been there in years."

"Yeah, well…now I don't really have any choice, do I? Dad is still in Costa Rica, and I don't know the next time he's planning on coming back, so I've got to be there to represent the ranch. And I think Emma would enjoy the trip to Tennessee, so yeah, I'll be there."

"You're not nervous, are you?" Jake winked at me, and I frowned in response.

"Why would I be nervous?"

"Because," he began, pausing to spit on the ground. "Little Sara Waters is going to be there. I wonder if she is going to follow you around like she always used to when we were kids."

I rolled my eyes. "Sara Waters is thirty by now. I am sure she has got better things to do than chase around a nearly middle-aged man with his twelve year old daughter in tow."

"Hey now, don't write yourself off just yet. You're only a year or so older than her, right? I bet she would be champing at the bit to get a piece of a Killarny brother."

I shook my head and started off back toward the stable, Jake following behind me with Clement.

"Then she can have her pick of the other four. Hell, she can have both Stephen and Sam if she wants them." I stopped and looked around. "Speaking of that, where are the twins?"

Jake shrugged as he continued toward the stable. "Who the hell knows. They're out every night of the week. Probably still in bed."

I knew he was kidding about the last thing. If we had been taught anything as kids, it was that getting up early in the morning was the Killarny way.

"Okay, well. I need to go find them. I'll get back to you about the Waters derby. We need to talk about some logistics getting there, but it can wait until later."

As I walked off toward the other barns to locate my two youngest brothers, I couldn't help thinking about what Jake had said regarding Sara Waters. I hadn't seen her since we were practically teenagers. It must have been a decade or so. I wondered what she looked like now and if there was a chance that we'd get some time alone when I was at her father's derby in a few weeks.

GET A FREE BOOK!

Join my mailing list to be the first to know of new releases, free books, special prices and other author giveaways.

http://freehotcontemporary.com

ALSO BY JESSA JAMES

Bad Boy Billionaires
Lip Service
Rock Me
Lumber jacked
Baby Daddy

The Virgin Pact
The Teacher and the Virgin
His Virgin Nanny
His Dirty Virgin

Club V
Unravel
Undone
Uncover

Cowboy Romance
How To Love A Cowboy
How To Hold A Cowboy

Beg Me
Valentine Ever After
Covet/Crave
Kiss Me Again
Handy
Bad Behavior

ABOUT THE AUTHOR

Jessa James grew up on the East Coast but always suffered a severe case of wanderlust. She's lived in six states, had a variety of jobs and always comes back to her first true love – writing. Jessa works full time as a writer, eats too much dark chocolate, has an iced-coffee and Cheetos addiction, and can't get enough of sexy alpha males who know exactly what they want – and aren't afraid to say it. Dominant, alpha-male insta-luv is her favorite to read (and write).

Sign up HERE for Jessa's Newsletter:

http://jessajamesauthor.com/mailing-list/

www.ingramcontent.com/pod-product-compliance
Lightning Source LLC
LaVergne TN
LVHW011833060526
838200LV00053B/4005